Della

Denise Devine

USA Today Bestselling Author

A Sweet Contemporary Romance

Book One

Enchanted Island Series

Wild Prairie Rose Books

Della

Print Edition

Copyright 2025 by Denise Devine

https://www.deniseannettedevine.com

ISBN: 978-1-943124-48-0

Published in the United States of America

Wild Prairie Rose Books

Edited by J. A. Dalton

Cover Design by D. Meinstad

Della

Sun, scissors, and scandal—just another day in paradise...

Della Delaney arrives on Enchanted Island armed with a hairstyling grant, a suitcase full of mousse, and big dreams of running her own salon on historic Main Street. But before she can unpack her flat iron, she's already fending off public doubt that downtown can be revived, and a gifted local artist whose killer smile is more than a little distracting. Between opening a salon and trying to unmask whoever is attempting to sabotage not only her business but her future, Della is learning that love—and success—never come without a little frizz.

He's done with art, at odds with his family, and struggling with his identity...

After getting rejected by every art gallery in Miami, Logan Chandler returns to Morganville with a portfolio full of watercolor paintings and his morale so low that he contemplates quitting the art scene for good. Then he meets Della—an optimistic whirlwind of vitality and sass who's convinced that giving up is never an option. When he discovers she's caught in a tug-of-war between Main Street dreams and resort-town politics—with his own family in the middle—Logan is forced to choose between his family and the girl who stole his heart while making him believe in his talent again.

Let's keep in touch!

Sign up for *Denise's Diary,* my monthly newsletter at:

https://www.deniseannettedevine.com/newsletter

Be the first to know about new releases, sales, and special events.

Prologue

The Saint Paul Hotel, St. Paul, Minnesota

Late January

Some days, getting out of bed felt like Sleeping Beauty trying to wake up from her life-altering snooze. Today was one of those days.

Della Delaney groaned and dragged the covers over her head just as the adjoining door to her parents' hotel room burst open with all the subtlety of a marching band. In stormed her older sister, Christina, the new Queen of Snows of the St. Paul Winter Carnival. The jingle of her charm bracelet, a gift from King Boreas Rex, heralded her arrival.

"Rise and shine, sleepyhead!" she sang with spirited cheer. "It's Sunday and you're going to the King's Brunch!"

"Ugh. Long weekend. I'm too tired," Della mumbled into her pillow, barely awake.

"No time for excuses." Christina marched to the window and flung the curtains open like she was revealing a surprise prize on a game show. "It's already eight-thirty!"

"Okay, Cruella," Della mumbled.

Then, like a true villain, her sister ripped the warm covers off the bed.

"Hey!" Della shrieked, flailing to grab the blankets like they were a lifeline. "Give me that back!"

"*No.* Mom and Dad are ready and waiting to go. You were supposed to be up thirty minutes ago," Christina said with a disapproving frown. "You need to shower, fix your face, and pretend to be charming. Social hour starts at ten. Oh, and since you *are* a hairdresser, I expect you to fix your bedhead. Okay?"

Christina stood tall and regal, a vision of winter elegance in her form-fitting, soft ivory wool dress. Her coppery hair was impeccably swept into a thick cluster of curls and crowned with the official Winter Carnival diadem, a sparkling symbol of her prestigious new title. Her makeup, expertly applied, completed the portrait of composed majesty. But underneath all that queenly grace, she was still the same bossy older sister by five years. Not even a sparkling crown could change that.

Della sat up with a loud sigh. "Fine. But I'm not wearing heels. I draw the line at toe frostbite."

"Don't be dramatic." Christina tossed her a fuzzy robe. "Hurry up. If you're late, you'll embarrass me."

Fully awake now, Della glared at her sister. "We've been going non-stop since Friday night. I'm wiped out."

"Oh, poor you," Christina replied with a wry smile, her dark brown eyes flashing. "I've already given an interview and made a television appearance today. Stop complaining and get going!"

Della yawned and tried to gather her thoughts as Christina swept out of the room, leaving the adjoining door open behind her. From the other unit, a deep, polished male voice spoke about the current temperature, a clear sign that her parents were watching the morning news.

How Christina could be so chipper on such little sleep remained a mystery. Della was happy about her sister's success and wished her well, but becoming an integral part of the Winter Carnival Royal Family was

Christina's passion—not hers.

At the four-hour celebration on Friday evening, Christina was crowned Aurora Borealis, Queen of the Saint Paul Winter Carnival, and became an official ambassador for the city of St. Paul. People cried. Della cheered and clapped until her hands became numb. Then came the Royal Ball that lasted until one in the morning.

At the Saturday parade, Della and her parents stood outside for hours just to catch a glimpse of Christina riding past on the official Winter Carnival float with King Boreas Rex, both waving like royalty and somehow not turning into human popsicles.

She looked amazing, of course, Della thought with a wistful shake of her head. *I looked like an Eskimo with mascara.*

Today was the King's Brunch, thankfully held indoors. There was just one catch. She'd spend the morning fielding congratulations on Christina's big win and dodging that dreaded question: "So, are you planning to follow in your big sister's footsteps?"

I'd rather climb Mount Everest in flip-flops than speak in front of a crowd of strangers, she thought glumly. More than anything, she wanted to step out of Christina's shadow. She wanted to stop feeling invisible, like an afterthought, and finally live a life that was truly her own.

It's time for me to turn the page, Della thought desperately, *and write my own story.*

Chapter One

Minneapolis/St. Paul International Airport

Early Friday morning, late February

Della Delaney stared out the car window at the cold, dark clouds covering the winter sky, wondering whether she'd made the right decision or if she'd wasted her last dollar pursuing the wrong dream. Her trip to Enchanted Island would either be the most successful gamble she'd ever undertaken or the most spectacular failure of her life. Was the risk worth it? She sighed.

I'll never know unless I try...

"There's the Delta sign," her mother exclaimed as her dad drove through the busy airport departure drop-off area. "I wish Christina could have accompanied us to see you off, but she has multiple appearances this weekend out of town."

"That's okay, Mom," Della said, sighing inside with relief. "She's busy with her own thing." Christina had voiced skepticism about Della's decision to set up a business on a heart-shaped tropical island fifty miles off the coast of Florida. She didn't need any more of her sister's doubts echoing in her head today.

Dozens of red taillights shone through the congestion like glowing beacons. Bill Delaney maneuvered his way across two slow-moving lanes of traffic toward the entrance to the Delta check-in area and darted into a space behind another car as it drove away. He parked the car and jumped out to retrieve Della's suitcases from the back of the SUV.

Della grabbed her large carry-on bag and started to open the car door when her mother, sitting in the front seat, turned to her with a serious frown. "Be sure to give us a call when you land," Rachel Delaney said in a worried, motherly tone. She looked like a mature version of Christina with coppery hair and dark brown eyes. "And be careful with your carry-on bag. You never know what kind of person you're sitting next to at the gate. It would be awful if someone stole your phone or your laptop."

Mom, Della thought wearily. *I'm twenty-five, not fifteen. I know enough to watch my stuff.*

"Okay, I'll remember," she said dutifully as she zipped her pink hoodie and opened the car door, anxious to get into the terminal and be on her way. She met her father at the car's open tailgate.

"Geez," Bill complained as he hoisted the heavy black suitcases out of the car. "How much stuff did you pack? These things weigh a ton. If they go over the weight allowance, it's gonna cost you extra."

"Just making sure I have everything I need," Della replied with a nervous laugh. She'd packed her scissors, blow dryers, and the rest of her hairstyling tools along with a few outfits. She'd acquire additional supplies once she got to the island. For now, she had enough to get started.

Opening a new business so far from home was exciting and a little scary, too. She'd nearly changed her mind—twice—but her father didn't need to know that. If he did, he'd start second-guessing every little detail of her plans. As it was, ever since she announced her intention to go to Enchanted Island and start a hair salon, he'd been trying to talk her out of it. When that failed, he'd insisted on going with her to help her decide if the venture was worth it. *No way.* This was something she needed to do on her own. She vowed to herself to work hard, take things one day at a time, and consider everything with an open mind.

"Here you go, honey," Bill said and pressed a hundred-dollar bill into her hand. Her tall, silver-haired father smiled, but the sadness in his eyes mirrored his true feelings. "This is from me and Mom. Buy yourself something nice on the island."

"Gee, thanks, Dad! Thanks, Mom!" Resisting the temptation to cry and climb back into the car, she shoved the bill into her pocket, hugged her parents with a hurried goodbye, and hauled her suitcases through the automatic doors into the terminal, heading for the Delta check-in area.

Laughter and excited chatter from the early morning throng of hundreds of happy travelers echoed through the cavernous, two-story ticketing lobby as she maneuvered her way toward the kiosk to print her bag tags. After her suitcases were sent to be screened, she went through security screening and didn't relax until she collapsed into her seat on the plane.

"B-r-r-r," she murmured to herself as she stared out the window at the leaden morning sky. Large flakes swirled in the breeze and drifted softly against her window. Depending on how things went on Enchanted Island, this might be the last time she saw snow for a long, long while.

Reaching down, she pulled a sheet of paper from her carry-on and unfolded it, reading it for the umpteenth time with the same nervous excitement and anticipation she had the day she'd received it.

From: lcbrown@edo.ei.gov

Friday, February 10th

Thank you for your request to the Enchanted Island Economic Development Office's small business grant program. Your application has been reviewed and approved for a matching grant in the amount of $5,000. Attached is the official agreement with details specific to the terms and conditions of the grant, reporting requirements, usage restrictions, and the timeline for disbursement.

As part of the program, the Enchanted Island Women's Business Association (EIWBA) has assigned one of its members to welcome you to the island. Elsie Dubois, owner of Bella's Enchanted B&B, is looking forward to assisting you through the process. Her contact information is listed in the agreement.

Please accept my sincere congratulations, and do not hesitate to contact me if you have any questions!

All my best,

Ladonya Brown, Grant Administrator

Enchanted Island Economic Development Office

1000 Main Street #304, Morganville, EI 00500

Della had never been to Enchanted Island and had no idea what lay ahead, but it didn't matter. The prospect of living on an idyllic Caribbean Island with sun-kissed beaches, mouth-watering cuisine bursting with vibrant flavors and island spices, and warm tropical air instead of a cold, snowy Minnesota winter sounded like heaven. Her first order of business, however, was to contact Elsie Dubois to view the property assigned to her to set up her salon and make sure FedEx had delivered her customer products to Elsie's residence. She'd already decided on a name, *Island Glow Hair Salon*. In her mind, she visualized a spacious, light-filled salon with large windows, trendy music, and a chic, modern vibe. Putting together something that sophisticated, however, would cost a lot more money than the paltry ten grand she had. Her stomach lurched at the thought of failing.

Think positive! she thought stubbornly. *Besides, it's too late to turn back now. I've accepted the grant, and they just shut the door on the plane. I'm on my way!*

Miami Ferry Terminal

Late Afternoon

Logan Chandler adjusted the nylon strap of his black art portfolio case as he approached the boarding ramp to the ferry, slipping the wide, flat bag over his head in cross-body fashion just in case he needed to make a quick exit. Over the past five days, hotel rooms, meals, and Uber rides to art galleries around Miami had maxed out the limit of his credit card. An hour ago, he'd paid for a burger combo for a homeless guy he'd encountered in front of The Shake Shack, and now he realized he didn't have enough money to buy a ticket to Enchanted Island. He was tired, discouraged, and wanted to go home, so he had to get creative. Looking around, he saw the perfect opportunity just ahead.

Short and frail, Dodie Pinder stooped over her footed cane in her egg yolk-yellow pantsuit, slowly shuffling toward the boarding ramp. Logan had known the dark-skinned, white-haired lady for most of his life. Poor Miss Dodie had suffered the misfortune of being his elementary school principal.

"Miss Dodie," he greeted in his most charming voice as he set down his other bag, a dark green duffel, and deftly slipped his fingers through the handle of her red, plastic shopping bag. "Let me help you with that."

She glanced up, a horrified expression crossing her face as she squinted to get a better look at him. "Logan? Logan Chandler? You give me that bag back right now!"

"I will as soon as I get you on board, okay?" He slid his arm around her waist. "Come along." He projected a concerned look at the employee scanning tickets. "Excuse us. My Aunt Dodie needs to use the wheelchair entrance right away. She's feeling faint."

"What? I'm not feeling faint," Dodie snapped, "and I'm not your aunt! I can walk up the ramp by myself. Go away, Logan. Wherever you go, trouble follows!"

The ferry employee, a tall, dark-skinned man with salt and pepper hair wearing dark slacks and a light blue, short-sleeved shirt, stepped forward with his portable scanner. "Yo' ticket please," he said with a Jamaican accent.

Dodie leaned on her cane, breathing heavily as she held out her season pass to have it scanned. Logan ignored the man and continued to move Dodie along.

"Yo' ticket, sah?"

Logan set their bags on the ramp and reached into his pocket, pulling out a wrinkled ticket from a former trip. He flashed it in the man's face and crumpled it in his palm. "I need to get my aunt settled first. Then I'll be back."

The man frowned, glancing back and forth from Dodie's dark face to Logan's light skin and blond hair as though not *quite* believing his story.

Logan responded with a carefree shrug, grabbed the bags, and kept moving until he escorted Dodie to a row of unoccupied wheelchairs. He helped her into the closest one and hoisted the bags onto his shoulder again. He quickly wheeled her to the security check and then to the row of handicap spaces inside the main cabin. "Here's your bag," he said to her and handed her the shopping bag. He pushed her chair onto an empty spot, locked the wheels, and strapped the chair to the floor.

"You haven't changed a bit, have you?" she snapped and snatched her bag, plopping it on her lap. "A spoiled brat who thinks the rules are for everyone else but you. And don't even think of sitting with me to keep me company. The next time you use me to get on board without paying, I'm going to report you!"

"You're right. I wasn't the most well-behaved kid," he murmured, "but even a brat grows up eventually. Thirty years will do that to a person. Believe me, Miss Dodie, I've learned my lesson."

The last five days were frustrating and depressing proof that growing up spoiled and wealthy didn't guarantee future success or happiness. Sadly, at this point, he had no clue what *did*. Pushing the thought from his mind, he walked away, heading for the lower level where the transported vehicles were stored.

He found an unlocked SUV and slipped into the back seat to change clothes. Pulling off his white polo shirt, he grabbed a black T-shirt from his duffel bag and a matching bill cap. He slipped on the items and completed his new look with a pair of blue aviator shades.

One long blast indicated that the ferry was leaving the dock.

Armed with his new identity, Logan left the SUV and stealthily made his way up to the main deck to blend in with the noisy crowd. The deep, methodical hum of the ship's engines reverberated through the floor, mixed with laughter and happy conversations of hundreds of passengers filling the wide, two-story room, making it easy for him to make the hour-long trip to Morganville unnoticed.

At the main entrance, the ticket inspector stood in the doorway, staring into the crowd. Suspecting who he might be looking for, Logan headed to the opposite side of the room to find a place to sit. Looking across rows and rows of bright blue loungers, he found an empty seat next to a pretty young woman who looked to be in her mid-twenties, with sandy-colored hair, and wearing a long pink sundress. The perfect cover for him. "Is this seat taken?"

"What?" She glanced at him, looking distracted.

"May I sit here? Or is this seat for someone else? Your boyfriend, perhaps?"

She pulled off her sunglasses and blinked, as though she had been deep in thought. "Um…no. I mean, I don't have a boyfriend. You're free to sit down."

She had the prettiest deep blue eyes, like one of the richest shades of sapphire paint he'd ever used on canvas. Her soft, sand-colored hair, accentuated with sun-kissed streaks of blonde, nearly reached her elbows.

"Are you getting off at Morganville or are you going all the way to Nassau?" he asked as he slowly sank into the seat next to her and dropped his duffel bag on the floor. He pulled off his portfolio case and set it on the floor, resting the wide, flat bag against the seat ahead of him.

"I'm going to Morganville," she said and stared out the huge window that overlooked the sea.

"Me, too," he offered. "I live on the island. Been there most of my life."

She swiftly turned toward him, her eyes widening with curiosity. "Really? Do you like it there?"

"I guess so. Never really thought about it before. Why do you ask?"

His gaze dropped to her pink-tinted lips as she burst into a generous smile, lighting up her face. "I received a grant from the Island Economic Development Office. I'm going to set up a business on Main Street!"

She looked so happy that he didn't want to burst her bubble. Most of the small businesses on the island failed because they couldn't compete with the trendy shops in the resorts. Sadly, once she'd used up her grant money, she'd find out for herself.

Despite his cynicism, he couldn't help smiling back. "So, you got a grant, huh? You're one of the lucky ones."

"Oh?" She looked so sweet when she frowned. "You sound like you're speaking from personal experience."

"Not really. It's just that most of the people I know who applied for one got turned down. What kind of business are you going to open?"

She gathered her long, silky hair and pulled it over one shoulder.

"A salon that specializes in trendy haircuts and other services like hair coloring and perms." She glanced at his art portfolio case. "What kind of business would you start if you received a grant?"

Logan sat back and drew a deep, tense breath. After the disappointing results he'd received this week, he had no idea. "I don't know."

She looked puzzled. "Well, what are you passionate about?"

"My paintings," he replied slowly, finding it painful to talk about. "But they're not very inspiring, or so I've been told."

"What?" she persisted. "By whom?"

He leaned forward and grabbed his portfolio case. "By nearly every art gallery in Miami."

"May I see one?"

He unzipped the case and pulled out the top watercolor, wondering why he'd just confessed his failed career to a total stranger. "This one is a wet-on-wet technique with painterly brush strokes," Logan said wryly. "One art dealer described it as a loose and expressive style…ethereal, dreamy, impressionistic. Then he went on to say that he wasn't interested because he already had a half-dozen like it."

She let out a surprised gasp at a picture of a pink-sand beach, palm trees, and vibrant buildings of yellow, aqua, and white on the island. "It's beautiful! You're a wonderful artist."

"Would you like to have it? Take them all, and the case, too." He let out a long sigh of defeat. "I don't have any use for them. Not anymore."

She slid the watercolor back into the case. "That's a terrible thing to say, mister, um…"

"Logan," he replied, removing his sunglasses. "Logan Chandler. And you?"

"Della Delaney." She turned toward him and placed her hand on his knee. "You can't give up, Logan. You're very talented!"

He didn't know if his talent was unique or a vain exercise in futility, but he couldn't concentrate enough right now to even think about it. The soft impression of her hand on his knee distracted him so much he could hardly breathe, much less think about the empty, meaningless future facing him if he gave up his art. "Ah…right," he said and quickly stood.

"Hey," someone declared from the next row. "Aren't you the guy who skipped out on paying for his ticket? I stood right behind you in line!"

"Well, I wish you the best of luck, Ms. Delaney," Logan said hastily. "It's been nice chatting with you." He slipped his shades back on, grabbed his duffel bag, and turned away.

"Logan, wait! You forgot your art case!"

Ignoring her pleas, he shuffled to the end of the row and headed for the upper deck to escape. He needed the sunny breeze and the soothing, peaceful view of the crystal-clear water to lift his mood. As he climbed the stairs, the salty wind brushed his face. The shrill cry of gulls circling the ferry cut through the roar of the waves crashing against the huge vessel. Alone with his thoughts, he leaned against the railing and stared across the shimmering turquoise sea, wondering if letting go of his dreams would make the ache in his chest disappear—or only make the pain worse.

He feared the answer.

Chapter Two

Della watched Logan swiftly stride towards the stairs, wondering why he'd abandoned his wonderful paintings. From behind, the sagging of his broad shoulders revealed more than he'd let on about his frame of mind. Why was he discouraged? So, a couple of galleries turned him down. So what? He surely had other avenues to pursue.

She zipped the art portfolio case closed, wondering how many months of work had gone into those paintings; how many other things he'd sacrificed to spend the time creating such beautiful art.

When the boat docks at Morganville, I'll track him down on the pier and return his watercolors, she thought, looking at his business card stuffed into a clear pocket of the case. *If I don't see him there, I've got his number.*

She checked her sports watch, anxious to reach Morganville. The hour trip to Enchanted Island had been underway for about fifteen minutes. She stared out the window at the golden February sun slowly slipping beneath the endless blue horizon like a liquid ball of fire, but she couldn't concentrate. She hadn't had anything to eat since breakfast at the airport, and her stomach growled.

Another fifteen minutes went by, and the aroma of hot pizza at the snack bar turned her appetite into a ravenous obsession. Placing the art portfolio case on her seat to save her place, she kindly asked the elderly, gray-haired woman two seats away from her to keep an eye on it. After thanking her, Della grabbed her carry-on bag, which contained her money, phone, and notebook computer, and made her way to the snack bar.

"I'll take a slice of cheese pizza, two cans of Coke, a turkey sandwich, one of those giant chocolate frosted cookies, and um…an apple turnover," she told the attendant, making sure she had enough for dinner as well in case the restaurant at the Amaryllis Hotel was closed by the time she arrived and checked in.

After paying for the food, she grabbed the handles of the thin plastic bag and started to turn around when she accidentally backed into someone who stood behind her.

"Hey! Way to go, stupid!" a rough, masculine voice bellowed behind her. "Look where you're going!"

Shocked at the anger in his voice, she whirled around and found a man who looked to be about thirty wearing a blue T-shirt and jeans, carrying a drink in each hand. He had short reddish-brown hair with a receding hairline. His closely cropped beard reflected the same deep color. Spilled liquor covered one work-roughened hand, dripping onto the floor.

"I'm so sorry," she replied, grimacing with embarrassment. "I—I didn't mean to spill your drink. I'll buy you another one if you'd like."

"Never mind," he grumbled as his grayish-blue eyes bore into hers. "My boss has been waiting too long for his whiskey as it is. No thanks to you, I'll have to drink the short one."

"Oh, but it's no trouble at all—"

His angry gaze raked her from head to foot. "Did you hear what I said? Quit pestering me and get out of my way. You *tourists* are always in a hurry." His lips twisted in disgust. "You get on my nerves."

He didn't have to take his bad mood out on her. "For your information, I'm going to the island on business. And you're rude!"

Suddenly, Logan appeared out of nowhere, still wearing his aviator shades and black cap. "Oh! So, here you are, honey. I've been looking all over for you." He hesitated briefly before pulling her close and sliding his arm around her waist, clutching her protectively. "Why didn't you tell me you wanted something to eat? I would have come with you and helped you carry the food back to *our seats*."

The firm but gentle grip of his long, muscular arm pulling her against his rock-hard body surprised her, causing her heart to thump erratically. She gasped as he tucked her shoulder in the warm crook of his arm and locked her in his embrace. He suddenly froze, as though he'd sensed a connection between them, too. "Logan? What do you think you're—"

"*Frat boy* is your boyfriend?" The man perused Logan with a derisive sneer as they faced off. He schleps beer at a local dive because mommy and daddy cut off his allowance. What are you doing with this loser?"

Logan's body tensed as he ripped off his sunglasses, his gaze zeroing in on the man. "She doesn't owe you an explanation, Bernard."

Logan pulled Della away from the counter and slipped his glasses back on. "C'mon. Let's get out of here before one of us does something both of us might regret."

"You can remove your arm now," Della said as he hustled her through the crowd.

Logan made no effort to let her go. "Not until we're safely out of sight. Vince Bernard is one bad dude."

When they reached her seat, Logan's duffel bag rested on the empty one next to hers.

She slipped her carry-on off her shoulder, setting it carefully on the floor. "Did we really meet by accident, or did you come looking for me?"

Logan picked up the art portfolio case and set it back on the floor, once again leaning it against the seats in front of them. "What do you think? You're new to the island. You don't know everyone like I do, and when I saw Bernard hassling you—"

His emphasis on "like I do" struck a nerve. "What's that supposed to mean? Are you saying that I'm naïve when it comes to handling myself around strange men?"

He shook his head. "All I'm saying is that most people on the island are fine, but there are a few bad ones that you need to watch out for, and Vince Bernard is one of them. He works as a maintenance man for a resort owner on the island whose reputation is worse than his." Logan picked up his duffel bag and slung it over his shoulder. "We're going to dock in a few minutes. I'd better get going. I need to assist someone off the ferry. It was nice meeting you."

"You, too." Before she could mention the art case, he'd vanished.

With a weary sigh, she sank into her seat and stared out the window, unable to get her mind off him. She knew plenty of successful, talented people, but none with Logan's gift. Those thick blond curls and hazel eyes didn't hurt either. The way he looked at her made it way too easy to forget why she'd come to Enchanted Island in the first place.

Get it together, Del. You came here to start a business, not to fall for a handsome island boy who oozes charm as easily as he breathes.

Dismissing the thought with a shrug, she dug into her snack bag, pulling out the pizza box. "That's just great," she complained as she opened the box. "I asked for a slice of cheese, and I got pepperoni. I hate pepperoni!" She ended up giving the pizza and the extra can of Coke to the nice old lady who'd watched Logan's art case.

She'd finished consuming the turkey sandwich and Coke as the ferry pulled toward the dock at Morganville, the capital of Enchanted

Island. Night had descended, giving way to thousands of lights dotting the jagged landscape across the island like giant fireflies.

Upon docking, Della retrieved her suitcases from the luggage rack and followed the crowd to disembark. Scores of people swarmed the brightly lit pier, catching rides or waiting for shuttles as automobiles and small pickup trucks lined up to pick up passengers. The balmy night air carried the savory aromas of jerk chicken and seafood chowder, accompanied by the laid-back, rhythmic groove of reggae music from the seaside restaurant down the street.

Della struggled with her bags, hauling them toward the express lane as she studied the long line of vehicles waiting to pick up passengers, wondering if any of them were from the Amaryllis Hotel.

She reached into her carry-on and pulled out her phone to search for the hotel's phone number. It didn't take long to connect with the hotel, but the automated voice that answered indicated the wait time to be approximately fifteen minutes. By that time, the pier would be nearly empty. She didn't want to end up all alone waiting for a ride! With a sinking heart and the phone pressed to her ear, she scanned the line of vehicles and the departing passengers who were travel-savvy enough to arrange ground travel in advance. Perhaps she could catch a cab.

"Della?"

Spoken from close behind, Logan's baritone voice startled her, causing her to accidentally disconnect the call. "Oh, no! I dropped the call! Now I'll have to start all over!"

"If you're calling for a shuttle, don't waste your time," he said as he strolled toward her. He'd removed his cap and sunglasses, revealing his wind-tossed blond hair and soft hazel eyes. "It will take at least half an hour to get here because all the resorts are on the other side of the island. Charles won't mind dropping you off at your hotel. It's on the way home anyway."

She peered past his shoulder. "Who is Charles?"

He gestured toward the end of the lane where an elderly gentleman stood at the open tailgate of a black Lincoln Navigator, stowing Logan's duffel bag into the vehicle. "Charles works for my parents. He's officially the groundskeeper, but he pretty much takes care of everything for them during the week when they're at the office in Miami."

Charles approached them. "Will you be needing a ride, miz?"

"It's Della," Logan said to Charles.

The elderly man extended his lean, dark-skinned hand. "Miz Della," he said in a gentle, fatherly voice with a Jamaican accent. "I'm Charles. Pleased ta meet you."

The kindness in his wizened eyes and the way he stood with one hand resting on Logan's shoulder—like a loving father—soothed her frayed nerves. "Likewise, Charles. Y—yes, a ride to the Amaryllis Hotel would be much appreciated."

Charles stared quizzically at Logan's art portfolio case sitting atop her suitcase but refrained from commenting as he loaded her baggage into the vehicle.

"The Amaryllis is about a half-hour away," Logan said once they were seated in the car, "but traffic along the coastal road is light this time of night, so it'll be an easy ride."

Della stared out the window as they pulled away from the pier and took the winding coastal highway. Logan immediately began looking at his phone. Della was tempted to do the same thing as well, but she kept hers in her purse. She'd never been to the Caribbean before and found the landscape fascinating. It certainly didn't look like snow-covered Minnesota!

They rode in silence, covering long, flat stretches of road along rocky shoreline and occasionally rolling hills dotted with the tall, imposing silhouettes of palm trees. A full moon hovered above the sea, its brilliant, silvery light creating a shimmering pathway across the dark, gentle waves. In the distance, a cruise ship, cloaked from bow to stern in a collage of bright lights, hovered like a giant beacon in the night.

The light from Logan's phone illuminated his face as he stared downward, captivated by whatever was on the screen. Della studied the thick blond curls falling carelessly across his forehead and noticed his frown as he concentrated. On the ferry, she'd curiously observed him, noting that his manners and protectiveness were effortless, as if second nature. The last time he left her, he'd mentioned that he had to assist someone off the ferry. Upon encountering him again at the pier, she'd sensed he had been watching out for her. Who was he really? After all, how many people had a chauffeur to pick them up at the pier? No one that she knew.

Twenty-five minutes later, Charles pulled under the hotel's brightly lit Porte cochere.

"Don't worry about your bags," Logan said as he opened the car door and slid out. "Charles and I will get them and deliver them to your room, so you don't have to wait for the bell captain."

"Thank you both!" Della hurried through the wide glassed-in lobby decorated with potted palms and ferns, wicker sofas and vases of freshly cut Bird of Paradise flowers to the registration desk to check in. She gave her confirmation number to the front desk agent, a short, dark-haired woman in a bright purple suit, and waited for the woman to access her reservation.

The woman frowned, typing furiously. "I—I can't find this reservation. Are you sure you booked your room with us?"

Dread flooded Della's mind, causing her palms to sweat. "Yes. I booked it directly through your website."

"I'm sorry, Miss Delaney," the young woman said. "I've searched our system, and it's not here. It must not have gone through."

Della shoved the printed proof toward her. "But I have a

confirmation number!"

The woman handed her the sheet back. "It's not in our system, and we're fully booked. I'm very sorry. I can try to get you a room at another resort, but I can't promise anything. This is the busy season, and everyone is probably booked solid."

"What's wrong, Justine?" Logan said to the woman as he and Charles came up behind Della with her luggage.

"Well," Justine said, looking upset. "I triple-checked and—"

Della whirled around so fast she smacked into his chest. Gazing into his eyes, she suddenly lost her train of thought. "I...um..." Backing up a step, her back bumped against the check-in counter. "Th-the hotel doesn't have my reservation even though I booked it directly online." Her voice wavered as she fought off tears. Now what was she going to do?

Charles glanced at Logan, conveying a silent message.

"Come on," Logan said and grabbed the handle of the nearest suitcase. "You can stay at my house tonight."

"No, no, I can't do that. I mean, I appreciate the offer, but I barely know you."

"Miz Della," Charles said politely, "we have a guest house that is rarely used, and it's completely private. No need to worry about it."

"He's right," Justine said, leaning forward across the counter. "Look, I feel bad that I can't help you, but if Logan is offering his guest house, I'll vouch for him. We've known each other since first grade. The Chandlers are one of the most respected families on the island. You'll be safe there."

Though it was an honest act of kindness, he'd already done more than enough for her. Not wanting to impose on him any longer, Della pulled out her phone and dialed the number for her mentor, Elsie Dubois.

After all, the email stated that Elsie would assist her with anything she required. "I need to check something first."

Elsie answered upon the first ring. Things were finally going her way. "Elsie, this is Della. Yeah, hi! I just arrived, and I wanted to check in with you." Elsie asked her how everything was going, and Della proceeded to tell her about the botched reservation.

With a sigh of relief, she disconnected the call. "Thank you for the offer, but you don't need to put me up for the night. I'm set," Della said to Logan. "Elsie's place is full, but she said she'd make room for me."

Shoving the confirmation printout in the trash can on her way out, Della left the hotel with Logan and Charles bound for Bella's Enchanted B&B, a colorful bed and breakfast on the edge of downtown. They had passed the large white building with aqua trim as they drove away from the pier. She didn't want to impose on Elsie, but she didn't have any choice. At least for tonight, anyway. Besides, she couldn't wait to meet the woman who had been chosen to help her get her business started.

After another ride halfway around the island, Charles pulled up in front of Elsie's place, Bella's Enchanted B&B. Logan opened the car door and assisted Della out of the back seat as Charles opened the hatch and pulled out the suitcases.

"Here you are," Logan said softly, holding her hand. The touch of his strong fingers curving around her palm rattled her so much that she bumped her head when getting out of the car.

He stood close, clearing his throat as though he felt as awkward as she did. "I guess this is our final goodbye."

"I—I guess it is," Della whispered, a wave of disappointment clouding her mind as she reluctantly pulled her hand away. "Perhaps we'll run into each other again."

"I hope so," he replied softly as their gazes held.

The front door banged shut, announcing Elsie's presence. A short woman with white hair wound into a top knot marched toward them with a wide smile on her wrinkled face. She wore a blue flowered dress, white duck tennis shoes with the backs trodden down, and knee-high nylon stockings rolled down to her ankles.

"Evening, Logan, Charles," she said in a strong but friendly voice. "You must be Della. It's nice to meet you." After a quick hug, she grabbed the handle of one of Della's suitcases. "I've brewed decaf coffee to have with a plate of fresh coconut tart. Do you like coconuts? The dessert is an island specialty."

"That sounds wonderful," Della replied, relieved to find Elsie so easy to talk to.

"Come along then," Elsie said as she began to pull the suitcase toward the front door. "Let's get these bags into the house. I've set up a cot for you in the gift shop." She nodded at Logan and Charles. "Goodnight, gentlemen."

Della grabbed her other suitcase, waved to the men and followed Elsie into the house, excited to get her new adventure started.

Flanked by tall palms on his parents' mountain view estate, Logan leaned his shoulder against the doorway of the small, shady greenhouse and peered inside, wondering how he'd collected so many supplies. For the past two years, he'd been using the narrow building with large windows and skylights as a makeshift studio. Scents of mineral spirits and linseed oil overpowered the lingering notes of peat moss and potting soil. Sunny wooden worktables that once brimmed with potted plants had been replaced with baskets of paint tubes sorted by color family and an old toolbox containing markers, pencils, Exacto knives, and scissors. The opposite workbench held several ceramic vases filled with brushes. A stack of blank canvases filled one corner. In another corner stood an easel holding a painting covered with a white cloth.

Soft footfalls swished through the freshly cut grass. He spun around to find his older sister, Michelle, coming toward him wearing a green floral swimsuit under a matching kimono and flip-flops. "Hey," she said softly as she approached, her chin-length flaxen hair glistening in the morning sun. "How's the packing coming along?"

Logan shrugged. "I'm working on it."

She approached the door and gingerly looked inside. "Looks like you've got a way to go. Mom says everything must be out of here in the next two weeks. She wants her greenhouse back. Where are you going to store all this stuff? You can't put it in the garage."

Rubbing the back of his neck, he let out a tense sigh. "I don't know. It just might all go in the trash." He grabbed the art portfolio case that Della had insisted he take back last night and pulled out the watercolor paintings. "You want any of these? Last chance before they get tossed."

She folded her arms and leaned her slender body against the weathered wooden doorframe, staring at him in annoyance. "Don't get dramatic. Mom and Grant aren't kicking you out of here because they're against your art. It's a nice hobby. They're just concerned about your future. I mean, you hide yourself away in this hothouse for hours every day. It's become an obsession with you. Meanwhile, your accounting license is going to waste."

"My license was a mistake," Logan argued. "I don't want to spend the rest of my life working for Mom and Grant doing corporate taxes like you and Jon. It's boring and predictable and demanding. If I could do it all over again, I'd major in art history instead of letting them talk me into something that I learned to hate."

"It's good money, Logan."

"Money isn't everything, Michelle."

"Without it, you can't do anything, and that includes playing all day with your paints." She pushed herself away from the doorframe and turned to leave. "One day you'll wake up and realize that the best part of your life is gone, and you're broke, but by then it'll be too late."

Logan shoved the watercolors back into the case and tossed the case aside. "Too late for what? Hemorrhoids and back pain from sitting hunched over a computer all day, filling in forms? Give me a break. I'd rather be poor at doing what I love than working at a job where I spend all day watching the clock."

Since his sophomore year in high school, his mother and stepfather had groomed him to become a CPA, ready to inherit their massive tax firm alongside his siblings, Jon and Michelle. His parents meant well, but their relentless focus on passing down their legacy to their children left no room to consider that he might not share their dream. To them, his art was just a hobby, and a trivial one at that—but crunching numbers would never be his passion. All he'd ever wanted was to make the world come to life on canvas.

"I'm not going to argue with you," Michelle said as she walked away, heading toward the pool. "I just came to talk some sense into you, but I see that's not going to happen, so I'm out of here. I just hope that one day you'll get serious about your future and realize what a gift you've been given."

Ignoring her comments, he turned his back on her and stared at the mess, losing what little enthusiasm he had for packing up today. Why couldn't his family leave him alone and let him find his own path to success? Why did everything always come down to making money? His parents were consumed with the idea, and so were his siblings. Their constant pressure on him to get a "real" job instead of working weekends as a bartender so that he could paint during the week used to make him angry. Now he'd begun to wonder if they were right. Since his disappointing string of rejections, he'd begun to question everything...

"Hey."

Charles stood in the back doorway wearing dark slacks and a blue flowered shirt, the concern in his ebony eyes revealing that he'd overheard the conversation with Michelle.

"Maybe she's right," Logan said, picking up a brush and nervously tapping it on the workbench. "Maybe I should go back to working full-time with the firm and—"

"And do what?" Charles interjected in Jamaican Patois. "Struggle ta be someone you're not just ta please everyone else?" He gestured toward the covered canvas. "You're good, Logan. Don't sell yourself short. You've got what it takes to be a successful art-eest."

Logan smiled with gratitude toward the one person who had always believed in him. Charles had taught him how to paint at eight years old and had always encouraged him to follow his heart.

"You're a natural, son." His gentle, deep voice carried a note of pride. "I knew it da first time you picked up a brush, and I'm going ta prove it to you."

Logan dropped the paintbrush on the counter. "How? What do you mean?"

"Da LaBore Museum is sponsoring a juried art show and da entries are due on Monday." He placed his hand on the edge of the covered canvas. "You're entering your best work."

"No, not that one," Logan argued as he shook his head. "That scene is too controversial. I've never tackled something like that before, and I don't know if I've conveyed the message correctly. Besides, it needs some finishing touches."

Charles lifted the cover, exposing a monochromatic oil painting in umber and white. "It's perfect. Da message is clear, believe me." He dropped the drape and looked up. "I submitted all da required paperwork for you and paid da fee. You're in."

"Yeah, but Charles, the historical image that the painting depicts is of the LaBore family's working plantation. It's going to upset the museum's major donors, my parents included!"

Charles replied with a disgusted snort. "Maybe they'll see it for what it is—da truth about our history. In any event, da entries are anonymous. Only da coordinators know who entered what. Has anyone else but me seen this painting?"

Logan shook his head. He'd finished it a month ago, but no one in his family had seen it because they had no interest in visiting his studio. Now, they were kicking him out.

Charles replied with a wizened smile. "Then doan worry about it. When you make the final cut, your family will be so proud of you they won't object."

After Charles left, Logan pulled the cover back and stared at the stark scene of Jamaican slaves cutting sugar cane under a leaden sky while supervised by a European overseer on horseback with the LaBore mansion looming in the background. The only reason he'd painted this picture directly from the old daguerreotype that he'd purchased from an antique dealer in Miami was because, since the first time he'd observed it, he couldn't get the island's past off his mind. This picture really was worth a thousand words.

He dropped the cover back over the painting, wondering if it would even make it through the first round of judging.

Time would tell.

Chapter Three

Della woke early on the narrow cot that Elsie had set up for her in the small gift shop located at the back of the B&B. The little shop, formerly a porch connecting the house to the garage, was so crowded with tables and shelves of local handmade items that she couldn't move fast, worried she'd bump into something and break it. She found the little shop fascinating and wished she could spend all day browsing among the jewelry made from sea glass, painted geckos, and hand-carved wooden bowls, but getting started on her own shop today was more important. She couldn't wait!

Elsie provided a small buffet of American and Caribbean fare for breakfast in her lemon-colored dining room with white woodwork and matching sheer curtains. Della sat among the guests at the large wooden table with a plate of eggs, toast, and a slice of pineapple tart that Elsie had baked fresh that morning. Staring out the window at the palm trees shading the sidewalk, she sipped a steaming mug of Jamaican Blue coffee and curiously watched islanders and tourists leisurely pass by the house on their way to the water taxi terminal just down the street. Life seemed so different here. No one was in a hurry; everyone was on *island time*. They smiled and laughed as though they hadn't a care in the world. Slowly, all the stress of yesterday melted away, replaced by a calmness that she'd never experienced back home.

"I'm ready to take you downtown as soon as you finish breakfast," Elsie said, breaking into her thoughts. "James has already put your bags in the car."

Well, everyone seemed carefree except Elsie. From what Della had observed, Elsie ran her business like a military installation, barking orders like a five-star general to her daughter, Bella, and son-in-law, James. Still, Della liked the short, stout woman who wore her hair twisted into a white knot at the top of her head and respected her as a successful businesswoman. Elsie had come to the island as a young bride, but after her husband's untimely death, she had turned her home into a profitable business.

After breakfast, they set off for Mainstreet, a two-block area of historic downtown Morganville, to view Della's new salon.

"This is it," Elsie said as she pulled up to a row of two-story brick buildings sitting shoulder to shoulder along the street. She opened the car door and, with a grunt, slid out of the car. "The Morganville Hotel over there," she said as she pointed across the street to a huge pink building with white shutters and black wrought iron balconies, "is what started the restoration of downtown. When Shawn and Pete bought the building, they convinced the Island Economic Development Council to clean up the entire downtown area. They argued that they couldn't make a go of the hotel unless the businesses around it were thriving."

Della stared down the street, seeing only old storefronts. All empty.

"The Council upgraded the utilities and put in new sidewalks, restored the lighting, and the cobblestone street. Then they implemented the grant program to fill all the shops. You, my dear," Elsie said as she closed the car door, "are one of the first people to receive a grant. Congratulations!"

They stood in front of an old barber shop with wide windows. Next to the door, the faded barber pole had red and blue stripes in a rusty casing that didn't spin anymore, proof that it had seen better days. Elsie opened the front door and went inside. A small bell above the frame jingled, announcing their presence.

Della followed numbly after her, wondering what she'd gotten herself into. "Doesn't downtown have a beauty salon? I saw one in a couple of old pictures of Main Street." She walked into the plain, rectangular room with two vintage barber chairs, a chipped shampoo bowl, green metal cabinets, and a large mirror on the wall, all the while wondering why they were looking at this place.

Elsie set the keys to the front and back doors on a faded green Formica countertop. "The beauty salon used to be at the end of the next block, but the interior was in such bad shape that the Council gutted the building and remodeled it to use for something else." She checked her watch. "Pete LaMaur should be here any moment now. He'll walk you through the unit and answer all your questions." She made a sweeping gesture with her hand. "What do you think?"

Della stared at the worn, cracked tiles on the stone floor and swallowed hard to contain her disappointment. "It's—it's…"

The front door suddenly burst open and a tall man, mid-thirties, walked in wearing steel gray chinos and a white Nike T-shirt that accentuated his huge chest and biceps. His chin-length light brown hair looked like it could use a good trim, but the thick, windblown style looked good on him.

He smiled generously and extended his hand. "Hi, you must be Della. I'm Pete LaMaur. I own the Morganville Hotel with Shawn Wells. Welcome to the island."

"Thank you," Della replied, taken aback at the warmth and friendliness of the handsome stranger.

"I went through everything in this unit yesterday, checked the electrical and turned on the water," he continued as though he sensed her reluctance. "The barber chairs are in good working order, along with the shampoo bowl. The restroom is fully functioning. It just needs some paint and a good cleaning. Would you like to view the apartment upstairs?"

Della blinked in surprise. An apartment came with the barber shop? Maybe this wasn't such a bad location after all, she thought, warming to the idea of not having to pay rent for two places. "Yes, I'd like that."

Elsie waited downstairs while Della followed Pete through the back door to a small entryway and a narrow stairway that led to the upper floor. The plain, one-bedroom apartment didn't look much better than the first floor. The wooden cabinets were old and in need of fresh paint, the countertop was the same faded green Formica, worn green and cream linoleum covered the floor, and the once butter-yellow walls were scuffed. The white appliances, however, had come from a timeshare unit, and though they were ten years old, they were still like new.

"I'll need to get some furniture," Della said as she peeked into the small bedroom. This apartment needed a lot of work, but having a permanent place of her own made it well worth the effort. "When can I move in?"

Pete opened the door to the bathroom to show her the commode, sink, and a cast-iron claw-footed bathtub resting on a flamingo-pink tiled floor. "Any time you want." He flipped the light on to show her that it worked. "I could probably get you a bed frame and a mattress if you don't mind a used one. My business partner, Shawn, has access to a storage shed at the Amarylis Hotel that is full of stuff like that."

Her gaze bounced from surface to surface, taking it all in—the good, the bad, the ugly, but also the *potential*. "Sure, I'll take it— anything you can spare would be appreciated." She had no idea where she'd get the bedding to cover the mattress, but first things first. It was so hot up here, she needed a fan more than a blanket. "Can you bring it today? I'd like to stay here tonight."

"No problem," Pete replied and led her back downstairs.

Elsie slid off the barber chair. "Did you like the apartment? Are you happy with this space?"

"Yes," Della said with new enthusiasm, wondering how it would feel to soak in that deep bathtub. "I need to get my suitcases out of the car because I'm going to stay here tonight!"

Pete opened the front door. "I'll get them for you."

Elsie said goodbye with a hug and a promise to help her in any way that she could.

Pete hauled in her luggage and said he'd be back later with the bed.

Once they left, Della zipped open one of the cases and began to unpack her salon equipment, getting a feel for the space and what she'd need, or rather could afford, to make it her own. Through the open back door, she saw a sign on a building across the alley that indicated it was the back of a hardware store. Just the place to visit later to get a fan and a few necessities.

She was busy setting up her workstation when the bell on the door jingled. Assuming Pete or Elsie had come back, she whirled around. "Did you forget something—"

A young woman in her mid-twenties stood in the doorway wearing a long, off-the-shoulder dress in a bright orange print with gold jewelry that set off her smooth caramel skin and matching melon-colored lipstick. Long black cornrows framed her oval face and sleek neck. Her wide, coffee-colored eyes glanced around with uncertainty.

"Hi," Della said, curious. "May I help you?"

"I saw Elsie Dubois' car parked out front, and I wondered if someone had already claimed this space," she said with a desperate tone in her voice.

"Yes, I'm moving in today. I've always had a dream of having my own shop," Della replied. "Now, it's come true. Did you get a grant?"

36

The young woman shook her head. "My application was rejected, but when my granny found out how disappointed I was, she gave me money to start a business without it. I was hoping to lease this property."

Della set down the curling iron in her hand and stepped forward. "I'm Della Delaney. Are you a resident of the island?"

"I'm Lainey Clarke," she said, walking toward Della. "I've been living in Atlanta for the past seven years, but I just moved back to the island for good. I missed my family."

"Your hair is beautiful," Della said, admiring her long cornrows. "Did you braid it yourself?"

Laney flashed a beautiful smile. "It's my specialty. I could do your hair like mine if you'd like to try it."

Della laughed. "It looks great on you, but I don't know how it would look on an Irish girl from Minnesota!"

Lainey stared at her open suitcases. "You came here all the way from Minnesota? Did you come alone, or do you have a partner?"

"No, I'm by myself," Della said. "It's crazy, I know, but I want to try something new."

Lainey clutched the strap of her fawn leather purse as though suddenly nervous. "Given that you have two chairs, I was hoping that you were open to adding an additional operator. Would you…consider renting your extra chair to me? We could work as a team. I specialize in hair braiding and hair straightening. I also do great nails."

Her question caught Della by surprise. She'd never considered having a partner. Just the same, the idea had merit. The business would still be hers, but renting out the other chair would bring in extra money. And perhaps bring in more business for both of them because Lainey grew up on the island. She probably knew most of the residents. There was just one catch. Provisions for taking on a partner after she'd received the grant weren't mentioned in the agreement she signed with the

Council. Was it allowed? There was only one way to find out. Picking up her phone, she called Elsie and explained her situation.

"Wow," Della said as she discontinued the call. "I'm amazed at how fast news travels on this island. Elsie already knew you'd come to see me and said there was no problem with bringing you on board. She said she goes to church with your mom and your granny and could vouch for your credibility. If Elsie approves, that's good enough for me. So, you're in."

Lainey burst into laughter and spun around. "Great! When can I move in?"

"Whenever you want to," Della replied with a smile, "but since I'm new here, I don't know what to charge you for rent."

"Let's go to dinner tonight and discuss it. It's my treat! I know a great place to eat where all the locals go. I'll call my sister at the FedEx office and ask her to make a discount coupon for us to hand out to potential new customers."

"Okay!" Della loved Lainey's enthusiasm and could barely contain her own excitement.

Lainey spun around, gazing at the room. "Girl, this place needs some work. These walls could use some color! We need to set up a trendy atmosphere with music, nice furniture, and maybe some local artwork."

"You mean like paintings?" Della chewed on her lip, wishing she'd taken Logan up on his offer. "I've got that covered. I know the perfect person to ask."

Della spent the rest of the day unpacking her equipment and making a list of supplies to buy at the hardware store to modernize the shop and her apartment. At noon, Pete arrived with a teenage helper to haul her new bed and a small dresser up to her apartment.

Lainey went home to get a few things and returned with a car full of small furnishings, bedding, and household items that her mother wanted to donate "to the cause."

Late in the afternoon, Della taped a poster to the window with her shop name: *Island Glow Hair Salon*. Staring at it from out on the sidewalk, the bold letters seemed to jump off the paper, and suddenly, everything seemed to fall into place. She couldn't help but smile as a small flame of hope burned in her heart. She was here. She had a partner. Her dream was real.

Taking a deep breath, she whispered to herself, "Here's to new beginnings."

As she turned to head inside, she cast one last glance at the sign in the window. It wouldn't be easy. Starting one of the first new businesses in an almost empty downtown area created more challenges than advantages, but this was her chance to succeed, and she was determined to make it work.

She stepped inside, committed to making her dream a reality.

Chapter Four

A balmy evening breeze blew through the open windows at Nigel's Bar and Grill, one of the oldest buildings on Enchanted Island. The barroom resembled a large beach hut with a gray stone floor, wide windows that overlooked the sea, and bamboo furniture with bright aqua cushions.

Logan moved from behind the acacia wood bar, juggling a trio of frosty beer bottles in sync with the tempo of a lively Caribbean tune echoing throughout the room. When the crowd began to cheer, he tossed them one by one to a group of young men at a nearby table, tourists from one of the resorts, who put on a show of catching them, making the crowd roar with laughter.

Forcing a smile, Logan performed an exaggerated bow. He'd executed the trick perfectly, but his heart wasn't in it. Michelle's words from earlier that day weighed heavily on his mind.

Mom and Grant aren't kicking you out of here because they're against your art. It's a nice hobby. They're just concerned about your future.

He understood their concern, but it bothered him that they didn't understand *him*. Painting wasn't just a fun way to pass the time. It was his life. He loved his art more than anything. Kicking him out of the greenhouse wouldn't cause him to suddenly see things their way. Why didn't they understand that it would simply force him to find another space to paint? He only hoped he could find one with as much light and character as the greenhouse provided.

Nigel, the elderly owner of the bar, sat in his private director's chair at one end of the long counter, wearing faded jeans and a red shirt printed with yellow sailboats. His dark skin glistened under the lights. His graying hair, shorn close to his head, matched his salt-and-pepper beard. Shaking his head at Logan's antics, he grinned in amusement, revealing a shiny gold tooth in the front of his mouth.

Nigel's catered to a lot of tourists from the resorts, but also residents of the island; a variety of people who came for the conch chowder and stayed for the entertainment. Of the locals who came into the bar, Logan knew nearly everyone. He'd gone to school with many of them and knew their parents.

He grabbed his audience's attention again as he proceeded to balance a fifth of whiskey on his chin. Someone sitting on the left side of the bar, wearing a Bob Marley T-shirt, hailed him for a drink. The guy looked familiar. Late twenties, light brown skin, thick black afro hair, and a thin mustache. Logan stared so long he became distracted and almost lost control of the whiskey bottle. With one hand behind his back, he snatched it from his chin with his free hand, tossed it into the air, and pivoted, catching it with the other hand. He set it on the counter to a round of laughter and cheers.

"Hey, Logan! Nice tricks. I never thought I'd see you working here!"

Recognizing the voice, Logan walked toward the stranger, an old friend from high school. "Tarone Williams? It's been a long time, buddy. Whatcha drinking?"

Tarone greeted him with a grin. "Gimme a Red Stripe. No glass."

Logan pulled a beer opener from his pocket, twirled it around on his finger, and uncapped a bottle of a Jamaican beer. He set it in front of Tarone and leaned on the bar. "I'm surprised to see you. Where have you been for the last ten years?"

"New York City." Tarone took a hefty swig of his beer. "I was a news photographer for one of the major news networks. I've decided to go freelance now." He glanced around. "What are you doing working here? Last I heard, you were a CPA working in Miami at your parents' accounting firm."

Logan shrugged. "It's a long and boring story, but one day I realized I never really wanted to be a number cruncher. Deep down, I always wanted to work full-time as an artist. So, I quit. This job doesn't pay nearly as well, but it's a lot more fun than filling out tax schedules. Nigel is a great boss. As long as I keep my customers happy, he lets me clown around as much as I want. The best part is that I only work weekends, so I can paint during the week."

"Really?" Tarone took another swig. "How's that going?"

"Things have hit a snag," Logan said, gripping his fingers on the edge of the bar. "I lost my studio space, and my parents are pressuring me to come back to work. I think they'd be more supportive if I had a few sales under my belt, but I guess I'm better at creating art than marketing it."

Anxious to avoid the subject of his slow-moving career, Logan signaled to a customer at the bar, sipping the last of his martini, to confirm if he wanted another one. The middle-aged man nodded in agreement. Logan performed a thumb roll with a silver shaker and set it on the bar, proceeding to pour the ingredients for a "dirty" martini— vodka, vermouth, and olive brine—into it. He finished making the drink, jammed a couple of olives on a stick, and dropped them into the glass.

The man shoved a couple of bills toward him. "Keep the change."

Logan thanked him appreciatively, rang up the sale, and dropped a generous gratuity into his tip jar.

"What brings you back to the island?" he said, turning back to Tarone and resting his palms on the counter.

"I got a grant from the Council to start a photo gallery," Tarone stated proudly. "My job has taken me all over the world, and I've amassed a huge portfolio of images. I've always wanted to sell my work to the public, and now I'll have that chance. There's just one problem, though," he said as he picked the label off the neck of his beer. "If I get called to work a gig, I'll have to leave immediately. I need someone I can depend on to mind my gallery while I'm gone." He stared at Logan. "What about you?"

"Me?" Logan stepped back, his hands falling to his sides. "I don't know anything about running a gallery. Why would you ask me?"

"You just said you lost your studio," Tarone argued. "You need a place to paint, right? I don't know how to run a gallery either, but I can learn. We both can. Besides, I don't mind if you display your paintings for sale alongside my images. It'll draw more people."

"I'd have to quit my job here," Logan replied skeptically. "I need the money."

"No, you wouldn't." Tarone nervously downed another swig of his beer. "You said you only work on the weekends. Just close the gallery early and go."

"Ah…I don't know," Logan said, staring at his hands. "I've got a lot of stuff."

"Not a problem," Tarone said. "I was already on the island when the grant offers went out. I got first pick of the spaces on Main Street. Of course, I took the biggest one," Tarone said with a grin as he leaned toward Logan and showed him pictures of the property on his phone. "My unit is on the corner with a two-bedroom apartment upstairs. I need one bedroom for a darkroom, but you could have the other for a studio. It's the biggest room, and it has a Murphy bed, so you could live there if you want to and set up your studio in the living room instead."

Logan mulled over the idea. It sounded interesting, but running a gallery could suck up a lot of time, giving him little freedom to paint.

Tarone shoved his empty bottle to the edge of the counter and stood up. "I believe the arrangement could be beneficial to both of us. Think about it, okay?"

"Yeah, okay," Logan answered, though his attention had suddenly zeroed in elsewhere.

Della Delaney had just walked in with Lainey Clarke, giggling as though she hadn't a care in the world and handing out coupons left and right. She looked amazing in a pair of red Capri pants that outlined her slender hips and narrow waist, and a white, off-the-shoulder ruffled top. She caught his attention right away, but something else pulled him away.

Like a bloodhound stalking its prey, Vince Bernard followed right on her heels.

Chapter Five

Della didn't know what to expect when Lainey asked her to have dinner at Nigel's Bar and Grill, but the moment they stepped inside, the magic of the island surrounded her. Through the wide-open windows, silvery moonlight glistened across the pristine waves of the Caribbean. The air shimmered with the melodic pinging of steel drums. Wooden ceiling beams were wrapped with heavy nautical rope, bamboo tables and chairs with aqua seats were scattered beneath ceiling fans that silently stirred the fragrant breeze. Her gaze drifted to the faux thatched roofing above the bar, and as her eyes adjusted to the dim light, she blinked in surprise.

There he was—Logan Chandler—behind the bar, conversing with another man and looking far too good in that sun-kissed, island-casual kind of way. He glanced up. Their eyes met, and something in the atmosphere shifted. His expression flickered with recognition, surprise, and something else she couldn't quite put her finger on. She didn't know why, but seeing him again made her stomach quiver like a palm frond in the wind. Did he cause that, or was it just hunger pangs?

"Let's hurry. There's only one open table left," Lainey said, interrupting Della's private thoughts as she pointed to a small square two-top tucked in the back of the room. She motioned for them to make a beeline for it—then stopped short, her gaze locking on something past

Della's shoulder. Lainey froze, a suspicious frown darkening her face.

Perplexed by Lainey's reaction, Della spun around to see what the matter was and nearly collided with Vince Bernard. With his baggy green plaid shorts, faded tank top, and flip-flops, he looked more like a lazy beachcomber than a maintenance man. He'd taken the time to comb his short, reddish-brown hair and trim his beard, but no matter how easygoing he appeared, the sting of his ugly behavior on the ferry still lingered in her mind.

She placed her open palm against his chest to keep herself from colliding with him. "Are you following me?"

His eyes widened. "Who? Me? Uh-uh."

"Yes, you are," she replied, getting in his face. "You're practically breathing down my neck! What do you want?"

He responded with a wide grin. "Maybe I just want to buy you a drink to make things right. We sorta got off on the wrong foot on the ferry."

Really? What caused his change of heart? She glared at him, unimpressed with his newly found interest in her. "Maybe you were just being yourself."

"You want me to apologize?" He tried to take her hand in his, but she pulled it away. "I'm sorry I was so rough on you. I was havin' a bad day."

"It's not necessary," Della said, backing away from him. "I'm over it. I've gotta go before someone else gets our table, so—"

"Aw, come on, honey," he persisted. "Give a guy a break. I'll buy you one of them, you know, fancy cocktails with an umbrella to make it up to you."

"She said no!" Lainey moved close to Vince, her beautiful dark eyes on fire. "Do you realize this place is nearly full? If we lose that table because you're holding us up, you're going to get more than a break." She grabbed Della by the arm. "Come on, girl. I'm starving."

Vince slid his muscular arm between Della and Lainey, shoving Lainey back a step. "Are you threatening me? Cause if you are—"

"What yinna do 'bout it, bey?" Lainey's voice had shifted, her Atlanta lilt giving way to the sharp cadence of her native Bahamian dialect.

A small crowd had begun to gather around them, murmuring, urging Vince to calm down, but he shrugged off the hands trying to hold him back and shot Lainey a piercing glare, his eyes narrowing. "Call me boy again and I'll—"

"You'll what?" Della shouted, poking Vince's chest with her finger. "Look, we came here for dinner, not a fight, but if you don't get out of her face, like yesterday, I'm going to—"

"Hey! Back off, Bernard!"

The deep voice thundered overhead, cutting through the chaos and causing heads to snap toward Logan as he maneuvered his way through the crowd. At his side strode a tall, muscular man dressed in a faded Bob Marley T-shirt and jeans with closely cropped afro hair and a thin mustache. Logan didn't break stride as he turned to him. "Watch my back, Tarone."

Tarone responded with a silent nod, his dark eyes scanning the crowd for trouble.

Surprised by the authority in Logan's voice, Della moved away from Vince just as Logan stepped between her and her unwanted suitor, towering over him. Why was he always taking it upon himself to rescue her from this guy?

Vince confronted Logan with a forceful push, knocking Logan back on his heels. "Mind your own business, frat boy, or I'll have the bouncer throw you out."

"I *am* the bouncer tonight," Logan roared, his voice rough with tension. "Nigel has warned you before about harassing women in here. This is the last time. Cross that line again and I'll throw you out, banning you forever!"

Glaring into Logan's eyes, Vince rolled his shoulders and clenched his fists, as if to prepare himself for trouble. "You can try…"

"He's testing you, bro," Tarone said in a calm voice. "Don't take the bait."

"Whatever he starts, I can finish," Logan countered, matching Vince's forceful stare.

"Let it go, Logan," Della urged, sensing that the animosity between them had been brewing for some time. "He's not worth it."

"Coming through!"

Della stood aside, clearing the way for Nigel as he pushed through the crowd.

"Settle down, you two," Nigel said to the men in a controlled but authoritative voice. "There will be no fighting in *my* place. Ya hear?"

Logan let out a frustrated sigh. Reluctantly, he raised his hands in compliance and turned away. "Yeah, I hear you. But if this moron comes near Della again—"

"Logan, watch out!" Lainey cried.

Before her words were out, Vince whirled around, landing a sucker punch on the side of Logan's head. Logan staggered sideways, momentarily stunned by the blow. Then with lightning speed, he swung back, hitting Vince so hard the man fell backward on the floor.

Nigel grabbed Logan by the arm, pulling him aside. "Enough! Go back behind da bar and do your job!"

"Police! Coming through!" A tall, lanky islander pushed his way through the crowd wearing royal blue trousers with a gold stripe down the leg, a deep yellow, short-sleeved shirt with epaulets, and blue Nike tennis shoes. "All right, people, break it up," he said in a Caribbean accent, the kind that Lainey had described to her as Caribbean English Creole.

The officer shook his head as bystanders hauled Vince, groggy and disoriented, to his feet. "You again? How many times do I have to arrest you for disorderly conduct before you learn to behave? It's another night of sleeping in da cells for you!" He slapped a pair of cuffs on Vince.

Vince defiantly sneered at Logan. "This ain't over between us, frat boy! I'll get you for this!" he bellowed as a second officer shoved him toward the door. He snarled at Lainey and Della. "And you, too!"

Lainey stood with her arms folded, impatiently tapping her toe on the stone floor. "It's about time you got here, Duane," she spouted to the officer in charge. "He walked in looking for trouble. I was about to teach him a lesson!"

"Good evening, Miz Lainey," the officer said in a jovial tone. "I don't doubt that you and your friend wanted to give him a piece of your mind, but it's best to leave da situation to me."

He turned to Della with his thumbs tucked inside his heavily equipped duty belt. "Good evening, Miz. I'm Sheriff Duane Hall at your service," he said with a smile and a bow, pronouncing his title "Sher-EEF Dee-WAYNE. "I apologize for da intrusion. Meester Bernard won't bother you no more."

"Thank you," Della replied with a relieved sigh. "I'm Della Delaney. Honestly, if Logan had been five seconds later, I would have hit him myself."

Lainey cleared her throat loudly enough for everyone to hear as the crowd dispersed. "C'mon. Let's claim that empty table. Hopefully, it's still available."

"You go on ahead," Della said, scanning the area for Logan. "I'll catch up with you in a minute. I need to talk to Logan."

He stood next to the bar, pressing a piece of ice to the back of his hand. A large red welt covered the right side of his forehead. "You okay?" she inquired softly as she approached him, concerned over the red, swollen knuckles on his right hand. "That looks like it hurts. You need to have a doctor examine it."

"Aw, I'll live," he said with an embarrassed grin as their gazes melded. "I shouldn't have hit Bernard so hard, but he had it coming. He's been warned repeatedly about using the bar to troll for women, especially the ones who clearly aren't interested. You were just the last straw."

She leaned in, lowering her voice with mock seriousness. "I appreciate you stepping in, but next time? Let me handle it. I don't need a bodyguard. I can fight my own battles."

He perused her with a troubled frown. "I just thought…well…since you're from Minnesota and all, that..."

His explanation floored her. "Wait—what does that have to do with anything?"

He shrugged, looking sheepish. "You've got that *Minnesota nice* vibe about you. Don't get me wrong, I like it, but I was afraid Bernard would mistake it for *Minnesota pushover*."

She didn't know whether to be flattered or insulted. Deciding to place his reply somewhere in the middle, she smacked her lips. "Pushover? No way. You've never seen me at a Vikings game with my face painted gold and purple, cussing at the refs like my life depended on it. Or shoveling a driveway when it's twenty below, or driving to the store to get ice cream in the middle of a blizzard. A jerk like Vince Bernard does not intimidate me!"

"Hmmm… If you say so," Logan muttered, wincing as he pressed a fresh piece of ice on his hand.

Lainey approached the group, her usual smile curving downward in disappointment. "Someone got the last table."

"There is always room for one more at the bar," Tarone said softly.

Lainey spun toward the deep, velvety voice. "Tarone Williams? Oh, my gosh. It's been ages since the last time we talked. What are *you* doing back in town?"

He patted the empty seat next to him. "Have dinner with me and I'll tell you all about it."

Nigel stepped behind the bar and handed them each a menu.

As Lainey slipped onto the stool next to Tarone, Della leaned toward Logan. "It looks like your knight-in-shining armor duties are on hold," she whispered and stared at the growing swelling on his hand. "Why don't you grab a seat before you pass out from all that heroic effort, and I have to rescue *you*?"

Logan snorted in annoyance. "It's just a bruise."

She arched one brow. "On your hand or your ego?"

He didn't answer, but the way he grimaced indicated *both*.

Chapter Six

Logan left the emergency room of St. George's hospital expecting Charles to be in the waiting room, a small area with almond walls, beige carpeting, and fake leather armchairs, but to his dismay, he found his stepfather there instead.

Grant Montclair stood the moment Logan appeared, casually slipping his phone into the pocket of his khaki trousers. He smoothed the front of his peach linen short-sleeved shirt—a breezy designer piece that hinted at understated wealth. A successful man in his mid-sixties, Grant looked impressively fit, the kind of person who ran miles at dawn or swam laps with the discipline of a former athlete. Though gray and thinning, he kept his hair neatly styled. His steel-blue eyes held the sharpness of a man used to being in control.

He stared at the cast on Logan's wrist. "What happened to you? Charles said you'd injured your hand, but he didn't tell me you'd broken it."

"A customer became unruly. I had to step in." Logan stilled, struggling to keep his disappointment in check. Grant was the last person he wanted to see tonight. "It's just a hairline fracture. The doc says I'll need to wear the cast for six to eight weeks, depending on how fast I heal. I didn't know you were back from Miami. Why didn't Charles come for me?"

"It's his night off, so I told him not to bother," Grant replied sternly. "But you'd know that if you were home more often on the weekends."

Logan stiffened at the disapproving tone in Grant's voice. "I work weekends. You know that."

"At a job you're so overqualified for that it's ridiculous," Grant argued as they began to walk toward the glass front doors.

Here it comes, Logan thought dismally. *The same old lecture... Ruining my life slinging drinks at a bar, and wasting my education painting all week instead of helping the family firm chase the almighty buck.*

"C'mon, Grant, don't start on me about that," Logan said quietly. "Bartending is only for now. Someday, when my paintings start to sell, I'll focus on my art full time."

That is, if I get a miracle, he added silently, the thought heavy with doubt.

"This is crazy, Logan," Grant said, shaking his head in frustration as he opened the door and stepped aside for Logan to pass through first. "What about your education? What about all the years you spent studying for your degree? We paid a lot of money to send you to the best schools. Are you just going to let that go to waste?"

"Going to college wasn't a waste," Logan said. "I don't regret that. It's an asset to my success, no matter what I do for a living. Becoming a CPA, though, *was* a mistake. It was always more yours and Mom's dream than mine. I'm sorry, but that's just the way I feel."

"What about your mother?" Grant pulled his key fob from his pocket and unlocked the black Navigator. "Barbara doesn't understand why you're letting your life drift without direction. You're breaking her heart."

Logan stopped at the passenger side, resting his hands on the roof of the car as he stared at his stepfather. "What about my heart? Don't my feelings count? My art *is* my life. Mom doesn't understand that. Neither do you."

Grant threw open the car door. "We understand that you're literally throwing the best years of your life away painting silly pictures!"

Logan yanked open his door and dropped onto the cool leather seat, his temper flaring. "They're not silly pictures! They're paintings—in watercolor and oil. Maybe if you'd come to my studio once in a while to see my work, you'd understand how important it is to me."

"Look, I'm sorry for sounding so critical," Grant said gently, obviously to ease the tension between them. He shut his door, fastened his seat belt, and started the engine before he turned back to Logan. "I've seen your paintings, and I'll admit—they're very good. You've got great talent, son, but you can't live on talent alone. You need a living wage job."

The shift in Grant's voice made Logan tense. He knew that tone. It meant that a pitch was coming. One where the word *no* never produced an acceptable outcome. At least, when it came to Grant's expectations, anyway.

"You're going to be out of work at Nigel's for a month or two," Grant said as he backed out of his parking space. "Why don't you put some time in at the office? Just a couple of days a week. We could really use your help right now."

"Grant, my right hand is in a cast. I can't do anything with it."

Grant sped the car across the nearly empty parking lot. "You can manage the service counter. That would free up an employee to handle more important tasks."

There it was: the offer of a seemingly easy job at the firm. A couple of days a week, managing the counter where clients dropped off their tax documents to be processed, and later returning to sign the paperwork to have their forms digitally filed. Simple enough—except that it wouldn't last for more than a day or two. Soon, he'd be shifted to another task, and another until he found himself back at a desk, preparing taxes—the very thing he despised.

"I'm not interested." Logan looked away, knowing his answer wasn't what Grant wanted to hear.

Grant pulled out onto the coastal highway and stepped on the gas. "It's your decision, Logan, but some choices result in undesirable consequences. Your mother and I have decided that either you get a job or you move out of our house and live on your own. You're thirty years old. We're not going to continue to provide a roof over your head for free any longer."

Struggling to control his temper, Logan turned away and stared out the window into the dark. First, they demanded he move his art supplies out of the greenhouse. Now the pressure was on him to *work for us or get out*. That was their plan all along. Get him back to the firm. Get a return on the money they'd poured into his education.

Grant was right. It was time to go. He should have moved out a long time ago, but he'd stayed on to be close to Charles, the one person who had believed in him, who had nurtured him from a fledgling to a mature artist. The only person who really cared about his passion.

Maybe this shove from the nest was what he needed to reaffirm his commitment to painting full-time and learning how to sell his art. No matter what he'd been telling himself, or anyone else for that matter, deep down he knew he didn't want to abandon his art.

Tarone's offer was still on the table. If he accepted it, he'd have a place to stay and a real studio to seriously pursue his career. When Tarone got called on assignment, he'd have the shop all to himself.

Suddenly, the idea didn't seem so bad after all.

Chapter Seven

"Yeah, Dad, things are going just great," Della assured her father on his daily phone call. Resting her brush on the edge of the paint can, she paused to admire her handiwork.

She and Lainey had spent the weekend painting and decorating. The salon now had a fresh, inviting feel, with three walls painted a soft, light green, accented by crisp white trim and a matching white ceiling. On the fourth wall, Lainey had applied wallpaper patterned with lush palm fronds, adding a tropical touch. A small CD player tucked in the corner played Caribbean music to lift the mood, and a pair of leafy plants in vibrant mango-colored ceramic pots brought the space to life.

"I'm just finishing touching up the woodwork, and then the salon remodel is done. We've added shelving and furniture. Yesterday we cleaned the windows and the floors. We're opening today. "I can't wait to get my first customer!"

Her smile faded as her father began one of his daily lectures. Today, he warned her about taking large bills.

"Yes, Dad, of course, I have my counterfeit detector pen. I'll be sure to check every bill in fifty and one hundred denominations to make sure they're legitimate." She sighed and rolled her eyes, hoping to get through this subject quickly. She didn't want to prolong the discussion by announcing the fact that twenty-dollar bills were the ones most likely to be counterfeited.

"I've got to go, Dad," she said quickly. "It's nearly time to open. I'll talk to you again tomorrow. Love you and Mom. Bye!"

Della picked up her brush and swiped the last spot on the doorframe. "All done and it looks great!" Blowing stray hair from her face, she bent down to gather up the plastic drop cloth from the floor.

"Our dream has finally come true!" Lainey exclaimed with excitement. "I told everyone at Nigel's on Friday night that we'd be open for business by ten o'clock on Monday morning." She glanced at her fitness watch. "That's in approximately thirty minutes." She glanced around, her joy turning to sudden panic. "Girl, we still need to organize our hair products on the display shelves and unpack our new supplies!"

Della put the lid on the empty paint can and began to quickly gather her painting materials. "I'll get rid of this stuff so we can finish up. We'll be ready by ten!"

At ten o'clock, she set the "Open for Business" poster in the window and propped open the front door, letting music spill into the street like a personal invitation. But there was no line of eager customers waiting to get in, no cars parked along the newly restored cobblestone street. Aside from a few guests drifting in and out of the Morganville Hotel across the street, the downtown area looked deserted. Dark clouds covered the sky.

"I wonder if people are staying home because of the storm," she said, glancing upward.

"Let's celebrate anyway," Lainey said cheerfully as she handed Della a bottle of chilled water. She eased into the chair of her small manicure table, turned on the bright desk light, and checked her makeup in the tabletop mirror. "I told all my cousins and everybody in my mom's Bible study at church about our salon. Don't worry. They'll come."

"Maybe we should have put an ad in the island paper," Della said, disappointment threading her voice as she settled into her faded green barber chair. "And include our discount coupon."

"Oh, totally," Lainey replied, staring into the mirror as she touched up her burgundy lipstick. "The paper comes out on Fridays. I'll hop online and set it up today. Did you know the island has a neighborhood Facebook page? I'll post the coupon there, too, and announce that we're officially open." She grabbed her iPad and started searching for the page. "Oh, guess what? Tarone is opening his photo gallery today," she said casually as she scrolled.

Della perked up. "He got a grant as well? I wasn't aware of any other businesses starting up yet, but ours. Main Street is so quiet."

"Yeah," Lainey said, tapping away. "His shop is at the other end of Main Street. And get this—Logan is going to co-manage the gallery with him."

Della looked up in surprise. "Really? He never said anything to me about it on Friday night, but I guess he was in too much pain at the time to think about anything else."

"He hadn't made up his mind yet." Lainey set her tablet back on the table, her long nails clicking on the keyboard as she keyed in the information with both hands. "But according to Tarone, Logan is moving in this morning, and he's taking the apartment that comes with the gallery." She paused, a troubled frown shadowing the graceful contours of her face. "Tarone's space must be a lot larger than ours because it's on the corner and it has two bedrooms. Apparently, nearly everything in it is brand new. They didn't even have to paint or clean."

Della took a swig of her water and replaced the cap as she mulled over Lainey's news. "That's not fair! When we close for lunch, maybe we should walk down there and check it out."

"That's what I was thinking, too." Lainey paused typing, giving Della a conspiratorial grin. "Are you sure it's the property that you're curious about or a certain handsome painter?"

"Don't be ridiculous. I'm just checking out the competition," Della countered, but her nervous laugh made her sound guilty as charged.

By noon, they still hadn't seen their first customer. Della placed the "Be Back at 1 PM" sign in the window and shut the door of the shop, locking it. She dropped the keys into her shoulder strap purse. "On which corner is Tarone's gallery located, Lainey?"

Lainey pointed toward the west. "It's a block and a half that way, on the edge of downtown."

Della glanced the opposite way, toward the east. Beyond their block, she saw a tree-lined walkway to the city park, Elsie's white and aqua B&B, and farther on, the long, covered dock of the water taxi terminal. She pointed toward the lonely shop on the corner nearest to them, one of the few remaining businesses to survive the road closure when the government repaved the street and sidewalks. "Whose shop is that on the corner?"

Lainey glanced toward the small, but beautifully crafted sign garnished with shells and colorful pieces of sea glass above the door. "That's Shakara Allain-LaMaur's workshop. She makes the most exquisite jewelry using materials from the Caribbean. Her stuff is so popular that she sells it on consignment in most of the resort gift shops. That's why her business lasted when everyone else's folded. She's also married to Pete LaMaur. They co-own the Morganville Hotel with Shawn Wells and his wife, Lisa."

Della studied the sign with great interest. "Really? I'd like to meet Shakara. Maybe she can give us some ideas on how to bring in customers!"

Lainey turned away from Shakara's shop and began walking toward Tarone's place. "Well, she *is* the president of the Island Women's Business League. We should go over there to see her sometime soon. I'll introduce you and ask her for information to join the league." She grinned. "But I've gotta warn you. Her creations are amazing. Irresistible even. You *will* buy something before you leave."

They shared a laugh and strolled past the vacant storefronts along the street until they reached the gallery. The old-fashioned bell above the door jingled a cheerful chime as they stepped into a spacious room with cream walls, large windows, and a sleek, dark tiled floor. Around the showroom, a curated mix of tables and easels showcased Tarone's striking photos on canvas alongside Logan's bold, expressive paintings depicting the natural beauty of the Caribbean Islands. Della glanced around, filled with admiration at the stunning display.

Logan stood behind a long counter, focusing on a project at a wide worktable. He looked up as they entered, his eyes widening with surprise as his gaze locked with Della's. A brief smile tugged at the corners of his mouth. "Hey," he said softly. "It's good to see you."

She suddenly realized how good it was to see him too.

Chapter Eight

Logan and Tarone designed their gallery to serve as an unapologetic reflection of themselves—bold, soulful, and quietly rebellious. Their space had an industrial charm, with exposed brick walls and black steel beams framing the ceiling. A mix of warm lighting and natural sunlight filtered through tall windows, creating shifting shadows that danced across the polished wood floors. Logan had arranged his paintings in clusters, each one telling its own story.

Interspersed among them were Tarone's black-and-white photographs—raw, intimate glimpses of life in some of the world's harshest places. Some were framed in weathered wood. Others were left unframed, pinned with care on thick display boards, as if inviting imperfection into the conversation.

A playlist of soft acoustic guitar and mellow jazz played low in the background. The entire space felt less like a gallery and more like a creative sanctuary—personal, grounded, and brimming with emotion.

Logan wandered among the displays and paused to study a large photo printed on canvas. It depicted a dark-skinned child squatting in a body of water. "Where did you take this?" he asked Tarone.

Tarone glanced at the canvas. "In the Congo. We were doing a story on child slavery." He pointed to the little boy. "He's panning for diamonds."

Logan stared at the photo, overwhelmed by the scene of the slave child.

"Photography is a powerful means of communication," Tarone said. "It exposes truths and conveys emotion in ways that words can't." He reached out and straightened the canvas. "That's why I take shots like this. I want to show the world that for many people, life isn't always a comfortable lounger on the patio with an ice-cold beer. It can be brutal. And it often is."

Tarone pointed toward another shot of children digging through garbage in India. "Many people are shocked into understanding just how dire some places are. It makes them think. It makes them feel." He shook his head. "I hope it results in making them *care*."

Suddenly, Logan realized why he'd been drawn to the picture of slaves working the sugar cane fields at the LaBore plantation. It's why he'd purchased the original daguerreotype image from an antique dealer and reproduced it on canvas. Because it spoke to him in a powerful way. And he hoped that by entering it into the art show at the museum, it would succeed in touching the hearts and minds of the people who viewed it as well.

"I'd like to show you something," he said to Tarone and went into the back hallway, retrieving his black art portfolio case from the coat closet under the stairway. He came back into the gallery and unzipped it, pulling out the canvas of the sugar cane fields that used to exist on the island. "I painted this from an old image. I don't know who took it, but I found the daguerreotype online through an antique dealer in the States who specializes in old photographs."

Tarone let out a low whistle. "Nice work. You captured the brutality of the scene perfectly. Are you going to display it in the gallery? Or don't you want to sell this one?"

Logan set it on an empty easel and stood back. "I've entered it into the juried art show that's going on at the museum. Actually, Charles entered it for me. I didn't think it was ready, but he did." He grinned. "He filled out the paperwork, paid the fee, and told me I had no choice in the matter."

"He's a good man," Tarone said. "He's like a father to you, isn't he?"

And he always has been, Logan thought pensively as he nodded in agreement. He carefully slid the painting back into the portfolio case and rezipped it. "It's due today. He's stopping by to pick it up." He went back to the hallway to return the painting to the closet, but paused in the doorway. "Entrants are anonymous until the awards ceremony. Only the committee knows who they are, so don't tell anyone about this."

Tarone agreed and went upstairs. Logan returned to the sign he was preparing for the front of the building. He nearly dropped his paintbrush in surprise when Della and Lainey burst through the front door, smiling and laughing. The cloudy day suddenly turned sunny—for him.

Lainey looked bright in a peach jumpsuit with a wide strap over one shoulder that tied in a bow. Della wore a long blue paisley dress, sleeveless with a low neckline and a large, ruffled hem at the ankle.

Logan swallowed hard and forced himself not to openly stare at how the contours of her dress outlined the curves of her shapely form.

"Congratulations!" Lainey said in a burst of enthusiasm. "This place looks great!"

He put aside his brush and stepped toward the counter. He had no idea they knew that he and Tarone were ready to open the gallery. Tarone must have kept Lainey abreast of their progress. "Thanks! Is your salon open now? How's business?"

Della and Lainey laughed at the same time.

"What business?" Lainey exclaimed with a smile. "Nobody seems to know that our door is open!"

"It'll take some time," Tarone said as his tennis shoes pounded heavily on the back stairs. He emerged into the room wearing jeans and a white T-shirt. "We need more vendors to draw people. My mom said that once Main Street starts filling up with shops, the town council is going to put up a huge sign at the pier to draw tourists here and plan events to draw interest from the islanders as well."

The moment Tarone's eyes met Lainey's, they softened, locking onto hers like they were the only two people in the room. "How you doin', babe?" he asked, his voice low and velvety.

She moved toward him as though they were drawn together by invisible magnets. "Better than ever, now."

He grinned and slipped an arm around her shoulders. "Want to see my new darkroom? It's upstairs."

They disappeared up the stairs, leaving Della and Logan with a sudden, awkward silence.

Della looked down quickly, her gaze landing on a long piece of plywood stretched across a table. The words "Main Street Gallery" had been sketched on it. "What are you drawing there?"

"I'm making a temporary sign," Logan replied, thankful to be discussing anything other than Tarone's new obsession with Lainey Clarke. He'd talked about her nonstop since the night they ran into each other at Nigel's. "At least, until we can afford to order a backlit one."

She suddenly gasped at the cast covering his right hand. "Oh, my gosh—your hand! You must have hit Vince Bernard harder than you thought! Does it hurt?"

"Not much," he said, holding it up, "but it itches like crazy."

She moved closer to examine it. "Buy a nail file. That would slip easily under the cast."

"I found something even better," he said playfully and pulled a thin piece of silver metal from his pocket. "Tarone's granny gave me a skinny crochet hook. Works like a charm." He shoved it back into his pocket and held up his hand with the cast. "It's hard to paint with this thing on, but I'm making progress."

"Why didn't you tell me you were going into business with Tarone? she asked, sounding hurt. "Lainey seemed to know all about it."

"Hey, I'm sorry," he said softly, feeling guilty. "I should have told you, but it all happened so fast, I didn't think about telling anyone. When Tarone approached me about it, I turned him down, but since then, my circumstances have changed."

She moved closer. "What circumstances?"

"Um…" The scent of her soft perfume distracted him. It reminded him of the exotic flowers in his mother's flower beds. "I've had a falling out with my parents," he replied, releasing a long, tense sigh. "My family… They've never taken my art seriously. My parents are still upset that I quit their firm. They think I'm wasting my CPA degree, throwing away everything they've invested in me. What they don't understand is that it's their plan for my life, not mine." He shook his head. "They gave me an ultimatum. Rejoin the firm and go back to working side-by-side with my siblings, or move out and chase a dream they don't believe in."

He looked away, but his grim expression revealed frustration still simmering beneath the surface. "I chose my art without a single regret. And I'm not looking back."

"I know all about parental expectations," Della said dryly. "My dad's convinced I'm going to fail. He's never come right out and said so, but he calls every day and warns me about everything under the sun. He treats me like I'm a five-year-old." She met his eyes with quiet resolve. "I'm not going to fail. I don't care if it takes me until I'm a hundred, I'm going to have a successful business."

Logan gently placed his thumb under her chin to lift her face. "I doubt it will take you that long." He couldn't help but burst into a smile.

"I wish I had your determination."

She moved closer, tilting her head as her gaze locked with his. "From what I've seen so far, I think you do."

Her rose-tinted lips, curved into a soft pout, quietly dared him to close the space between them. His heart somersaulted in his chest. Sliding his hands around her small waist, he tilted his head and—

The back door creaked.

Logan reluctantly pulled away and spun toward the noise.

Charles stood in the doorway, calmly waiting to conclude his business. The elderly gentleman wore crisp dark slacks and a white button-down shirt. His closely cropped gray hair stood out against his smooth brown skin. "Do you have da parcel?" he asked in a deep, gentle voice.

"Yes," Logan replied, shifting gears. "I'll get it for you." He turned to Della. "Excuse me for a moment."

He swiftly walked to the coat closet, grabbed the black art portfolio case, and handed it to Charles. "Here you go." His neck and shoulders tensed at the thought of strangers judging his work. Would they be impressed, or would they consider it just a cheap replica? He decided not to care. He had all he could handle right now without worrying about something he couldn't control.

"Thanks," Charles replied evenly. "I'll be on my way then." He nodded in Della's direction. "Have a nice day." The door closed behind him with a loud click.

Della curiously stared after him. "Logan, where is he going with your portfolio case—"

"I have a gift for you," Logan said quickly to steer the conversation in a new direction. He reached for a stack of framed paintings leaning against the wall and grabbed two of them, placing them on a nearby table.

"These are to hang in your salon. Or, if you'd rather, decorate your apartment with them."

"Thank you," Della replied in awe at the watercolors of the island. "These are wonderful!"

Tarone's huge feet thundered down the stairs, his tennis shoes echoing on the wooden treads. "Who was here?" Lainey followed closely behind him.

Logan spun around. "Charles picked up his package."

Tarone nodded silently.

Lainey and Della stared at him with curious looks on their faces.

Logan didn't elaborate, and for a moment, the conversation stalled.

Lainey raised one eyebrow. "What kind of package?"

Della tilted her head, eyeing him curiously. "And why did he look at you like the two of you were conspiring together?"

Logan responded with a tight smile. "Aw, it was nothing. He's just running an errand."

Outside, the hum of a car pulling away faded down the street, leaving behind a silence filled with unspoken questions.

Chapter Nine

The next morning, Della turned on the music and opened the salon, hoping to find customers eagerly waiting, but when she peered outside, the sidewalk in front of the building was empty. Where was everybody? Where were all the happy women who'd received discount coupons at Nigel's last Friday night? And the ladies in Lainey's mom's Bible study? Disappointed, she left the door open and went back inside to hang the framed watercolors that Logan had given her. Might as well stay busy.

A few minutes later, Tarone walked casually through the back door, greeting Lainey with a kiss and asking her to put cornrows in his hair.

Feeling out of place, Della gave the lovebirds some space and went upstairs with a fresh cup of coffee to eat a snack. Her apartment didn't have much furniture yet, but thanks to the hardware store across the alley, she had a small table and two chairs. She cut herself a slice of rum cake and sat down to eat it when the bell on the salon door jingled. Did Tarone leave? Why so soon?

"Della," Lainey called up the stairs. "You have a customer."

"I'll be right there!" Della cried, nearly choking on a bite of cake.

Della grabbed a quick gulp of scalding coffee, winced, and dashed down the stairs. In the salon, Lainey stood with a petite woman who looked to be around thirty, examining one of Logan's paintings. The woman had chin-length flaxen hair that framed high cheekbones, flawless skin, and wide blue eyes. Everything from her tailored designer outfit to her graceful posture suggested old money and confidence.

"Hello and welcome to Island Glow Hair Salon," Della said enthusiastically. "How may I help you today?"

The woman spun around. "Are these paintings for sale?"

"They're for display only," Della replied. "They were a gift."

"I see," the woman countered sharply. "I know the artist. He's my brother."

Della froze, stunned by the woman's frank admission. It almost felt like a warning…

"I'm pleased to meet you. I'm Della Delaney," she said carefully. "Logan and I are friends." Something didn't jive here. Logan's sister wasn't smiling back. Instead, she appeared guarded, cool.

"I'm Michelle Chandler." Turning away. She slipped into Della's barber chair, ignoring Lainey and Tarone. "I'd like a trim," she said, running her fingers through her hair. "More lift on the top." She met Della's gaze. "Can you do that?"

Feeling like her professional skill had just been insulted, Della blinked, fighting to keep her face neutral. The last thing she wanted to do was lose her first client. "Of course," she said, keeping her tone light. "How much would you like taken off?"

As Della began the cut, the conversation stayed polite but tense. Michelle asked a steady stream of questions about Della's background, what brought her to Enchanted Island, and how she managed to start a business.

The process took about thirty minutes.

"All done," Della said as she switched off the blow dryer. She offered Michelle a hand mirror to see for herself. "Is there anything else

I can do for you today?"

"How well do you know my brother?" Michelle asked, ignoring Della's question.

Della removed the salon cape and set it aside. "We met the day I arrived, but in the short time we've known each other, we've become good friends," she said, feeling a warm glow inside. "Yesterday, he gifted me the paintings."

"Logan's nature is to be generous," Michelle stated as she stared at the watercolors. "He's a great catch—but not right for you."

Della stepped back, floored by the statement. "What do you mean by that?"

"Don't get your hopes up," Michelle replied as she slid out of the chair and grabbed her Louis Vuitton bag off the counter. "My little brother has temporarily lost his way, but it's not going to last forever. When he comes to his senses, he'll realize what he's given up by leaving the firm, and he'll be back to salvage his career. My family has big plans for him. So don't get in his way."

She pulled a wad of bills from her purse and shoved them into Della's hand. "Keep the change."

Without another word, Michelle Chandler walked out of the salon, leaving behind an air of tension and three stunned people.

Lainey broke the silence. "Well…that was strange."

Della placed the money in her cash drawer and exhaled, frustration tightening her chest. "It sounded like a warning, didn't it? Why would her family see me as a threat to Logan's future?" She leaned against the counter, staring at the watercolors. "I have nothing to do with it."

Lainey exchanged glances with her but didn't reply.

"Oh, my gosh," Della exclaimed as she spotted a sparkling pair of diamond earrings that Michelle had set on the counter. She held them up.

"Michelle forgot these. I'll be right back!"

Della hurried out of the salon and looked both ways, scanning the empty sidewalk. Where could she have gone? She broke into a jog toward Shakara's workshop, hoping that Michelle had either parked around the corner or walked to the water taxi terminal. At the end of the block, she stopped to catch her breath, just in time to see Michelle get into a black Mercedes half a block away. A dark-haired man sat at the wheel.

Della stepped off the curb, holding up the earrings. "Wait! Michelle! You left your—"

The car immediately sped off before she could finish.

Disappointed, Della slipped the earrings into her pocket and walked back to the salon.

Lainey stopped braiding Tarone's hair. "Did you catch her?"

Della shook her head. "I just missed her. She drove away with some guy in a Mercedes, and they seemed to be in a big hurry." Reaching down, she opened a cabinet door and grabbed her purse. "I'd better give them to Logan right away so he can call her and tell her that he's got them. I don't want her to accuse me of stealing them."

Leaving the salon again, she headed toward Logan's gallery, earrings in hand. The sooner she turned them over to a Chandler, the better.

Chapter Ten

Logan stood in the gallery at one of the large windows, wearing nothing but a pair of Joe Boxer pajama bottoms, but passersby on the outside couldn't see him. Someone had sprayed all the windows with a can of fluorescent lime-green paint.

He fumed at the damage. It would take hours to remove the paint. Then he'd have to repaint the trim and clean the drips off the sidewalk. He wanted to smash something!

Tarone burst through the back door, cursing. "What a mess! This was more than a prank. Someone wanted to give us a message." He glanced around the room. "I think we need to set up a couple of cameras outside and at least one inside. High up so no one can disable them."

Tarone's phone buzzed. "Yeah!" he barked, gripping his free hand on his hip. "What? Lainey, calm down. Hey, if anyone is going to kill the perpetrator who did this, it's gonna be *me*. Yeah, they got us, too. On both sides!" He listened for a moment. "I'm going to the hardware store. I'll get enough remover for your windows, too." He hung up and shoved his phone back in his pocket with a wry chuckle. "She's *mad*. Remind me to never get on her bad side!"

Logan went upstairs to change and call Della. His phone rang as he reached the top of the stairs. It was Della. Her voice sounded thick, as though holding back tears.

"We can't seem to get a break!" she said, sniffling loudly. "The front windows of our store are covered in lime green paint! Who would do something so mean?"

"Hey, I'm sorry," Logan said gently as he slipped off his pajamas and pulled open a dresser drawer. "I know how you feel. We got hit, too. Our windows are a mess. Tarone is on his way now to the hardware store to pick up cleaning supplies. If anyone recently bought cans of lime green spray paint, he'll find out who they were."

He sighed, thinking about the mess. "It's going to take a while to get all this paint off because I can only use one hand, but as soon as we get our windows cleaned, we'll come over to your place and take care of yours. Okay?" Wedging his phone between his neck and shoulder, he bent over and attempted to slip into a pair of old jeans, but his toe caught on the seam, tripping him. Protecting his fractured hand, he landed on the floor on his back like a sack of sweet potatoes. His phone slipped away, skittering across the wood floor.

"Logan, are you there?" Della asked, sounding puzzled.

Reaching out, he grabbed the phone, then stood up with a groan and tossed the jeans on the bed. "Yeah, I'm just getting organized." Sitting on the edge of the mattress, he fell backward, stretching out on the soft cotton bedding, resting his injured hand on the bed. "Listen, I think we both know who did this. Bernard told me he'd get even with me, but he went too far by targeting you. When I get my hands on him…" He stared at his injured hand and let out a dispirited sigh. "Never mind. I'll let Duane Hall deal with him. Duane will be here in a few minutes to fill out a police report and take some pictures. When he finishes, I'll send him your way, too. In the meantime, I've got a lot of work to do. I'll call you and let you know when Tarone and I are on our way."

Tarone returned from the store just as Logan finished wolfing down his breakfast. He pulled on an old, washed-out T-shirt, slipped into a pair of old tennis shoes, and went downstairs to begin the grueling task of scraping paint off the windows one-handed.

They'd finished cleaning half of the windows when a silver pickup truck pulled up to the curb. Shawn Wells, co-owner of the historic Morganville Hotel, climbed out and surveyed the scene from the sidewalk. Tall and broad-shouldered, the dark-haired man wore worn jeans and a light blue polo shirt.

"Duane Hall told me about the vandalism," he said, expressing his disgust with a long, low whistle. "Man, someone really did a job on this place. Many of the island resort owners are unhappy that we're working to revive Main Street, but I don't think they'd go this far to stop us. This looks personal."

"Vince Bernard," Logan replied gruffly. "He threatened me the last time I threw him out of Nigel's. He's making good on his promise."

Shawn folded his arms, furrowing his brows at the accusation. "Is that right? Well, he'd better watch out. I have cameras all around the hotel. If he tries to hit my place, I'll know."

"I'm ordering a set for us today," Tarone said as he leaned against the pickup. "Unfortunately, the ones I want are backordered, but they're top of the line, so it's worth the wait."

Logan paused in the doorway. "Come inside and sit down, Shawn. We need a break anyway. Want a Coke?"

"Sure, I could use one right now," Shawn said as he followed Logan and Tarone into the gallery. He paused in the center of the room, slowly turning as he took in the scope of their work. "You guys do nice work." He walked over to one of Tarone's images, an aerial picture of Morganville. "How much is this? I'd like to hang it in the lobby at the hotel."

Tarone waved away the notion of paying for it. "Just take it."

"No, no," Shawn argued, raising his palms. "I'll buy it from you."

"You and Pete LaMaur have done so much to help us and all of the future businesses on Main Street get a decent start that it's the least I can do to return the favor," Tarone argued. "Help yourself. Take whatever you want."

"Feel free to take a couple of mine, too," Logan said, speaking up as he handed Shawn a chilled can of soda. "I gave Della paintings to hang in her salon. I'd like you to have some, too."

"I tell you what," Shawn said as he examined a vivid watercolor of Azure Bay, a scene depicting blue sky, towering palms and its incredible pink sand beach. "I'll take this one and the aerial photo in exchange for dinner at the hotel. At your leisure. Feel free to bring a guest, but all I ask is that you make a reservation so we know when to expect you."

Tarone's face lit up. He stuck out his hand to shake on it. "It's a deal! How about tonight?"

Shawn smiled. "No problem. Is seven o'clock okay? I'll make the call right now."

Nodding in agreement, Logan pulled the tab off his Coke can and swallowed a large gulp, energized by the prospect of asking Della to have dinner with him tonight. But for now, he needed to concentrate on the issue at hand. They had a lot of scraping to do at their own place before they could tackle the damage at the hair salon, so they needed to get back to work.

He wrapped the painting for Shawn, said goodbye, and went back to scraping.

A couple of hours later, Logan and Tarone arrived at Della's hair salon with a wheelbarrow filled with tools to clean the paint off their windows. The good news was that the girls only had two windows. The bad news was that Bernard had written an obscenity on their door.

"We'll take care of the door tomorrow," Logan said to Della as she met him on the sidewalk. She looked beautiful in slimming white Jeggings printed with bold green leaves and a sleeveless, square-neck top in solid green, flared just enough to catch the breeze. A jeweled clip swept back one side of her long, sandy-colored hair. "I'll just cover it with something for now. We've got some trim to repaint on our storefront, so we'll do both properties at the same time."

Della's deep blue eyes mirrored sadness. "Why not today? It's only two o'clock. I don't want our customers to see that."

Logan moved close, caught off guard by the subtle aroma of hibiscus. He drew in a slow, deep breath, momentarily distracted by the delicate scent. And by her.

"Logan…"

"Because I'd rather have dinner with you," he replied, his voice low and urgent. "Tonight. At the Morganville Hotel. Doesn't that sound like a lot more fun than slapping a brush on the door?" He smiled as he gazed deep into her eyes. "I'll pick you up at six forty-five. Lainey and Tyrone with be with us. Sound good?"

"Gosh," she said, nibbling on her lip. "What should I wear?" She looked up at him, her puzzled expression indicating she was giving the idea some serious thought. "Is the hotel restaurant formal?"

I'll take that as a yes, Logan thought, grinning in amusement. "It's historic," he said with a casual shrug. "Walking into the lobby feels like stepping back in time. It's grand in its own way. Wear whatever you want."

"In that case, I've got a lot to do. I need to wash my hair and do my makeup." Without saying goodbye or promising to return, she opened the door to the salon. "Lainey, what are you wearing tonight?"

"For now, I'll tape some newspaper over it to cover it up, okay?" Logan offered, but he knew her mind was already somewhere else. He watched her disappear inside the salon as a warm feeling spread across his chest. He had no idea what she planned to wear—casual or formal—but it didn't matter to him. He knew without a doubt that she'd be the most beautiful and captivating woman in the room.

Chapter Eleven

Della stood in the bathroom nervously fluffing her hair for the third time and checking her makeup in the mirror—again. Logan was due to pick her up any moment now, and she wanted to look her best.

What's the big deal, she thought to herself as she touched up her mascara. *It's just dinner with a nice guy, not a marriage proposal. Lainey and Tarone will be there, too.*

She paused, fixing a smudge on her rose-colored lipstick with her finger. Nice guy? She'd agreed to have dinner with one of the most handsome and charming men she'd ever met. Not only that, but Logan was also a gifted artist and super intelligent. Two traits that she found irresistible in a man.

"That's exactly why he's never going to get serious about a nobody from Minnesota like you," she declared to her frowning reflection. "He's an Ivy Leaguer who probably coasted into some prestigious fraternity—obviously—and that's why his parents are freaking out about the cost of his tuition. They raised him to focus all his energy on one purpose. To carry on the family legacy."

She rolled her eyes. "Never mind what he wants. They're probably busy arranging his engagement to some hedge fund heiress named Aurora. Or Jasmine. Or…I don't know…Countess Cashmere."

"Who are you talking to?" Logan called out as he climbed the stairs to her apartment. The kitchen door stood open, as usual, allowing the cooler air to drift upward.

"Um…" She blinked, embarrassed that he overheard her and racking her brain for an answer that wouldn't make her sound crazy. "I'm going over the list of supplies that I need for the salon."

"Oh," he replied, stopping in the doorway of the bathroom, his eyes widening as he took in her outfit. "You look fantastic." Taking her by the hands, he drew her into the kitchen and twirled her around.

She wore a short dress that she had borrowed from Lainey's cousin with spaghetti straps in deep blue fabric adorned with a bold peacock feather print. Delicate gold and crystal pendants glittered at her neck and dangled from her ears, catching the light with every movement.

Logan reached out, his finger softly brushing her skin as he gently tucked a stray lock of hair behind her ear, his touch lingering a moment longer than necessary. "Shall we go?"

Della blinked, mesmerized by the softness of his touch. "Um…sure." She slipped on her gold shoes, grabbed her clutch and a gold shawl, and followed Logan down the stairs.

They crossed the street to the three-story, flamingo pink building with large windows framed by white shutters and black, wrought iron balconies. The words *Morganville Hotel, 1861* were etched in the stucco façade between the top floors, proudly declaring its history. They stepped through grand double doors into a spacious lobby with a sweeping staircase that rose to the second-floor balcony, its mahogany banister polished to a gleam. The wooden floor creaked gently beneath their feet, and overhead, a massive crystal chandelier sparkled like a regal crown.

A gentleman stood behind a wooden podium at the entrance to the restaurant wearing a sharp black suit. "Do you have reservations for dinner?" he asked, his deep, melodious voice echoing throughout the room.

"Yes," Logan said casually, as if he dined at fancy hotels every night. "We're with the Williams party."

The man nodded and retrieved two leather-bound menus. "Right this way, please."

He led them through the busy dining room filled with soft voices and the tinkling of silverware on fine china into a stone courtyard framed by arched brick doorways and wrought iron balconies on the upper floors. Cascading vines of pink, purple, and white bougainvillea spilled over the railings, enhancing the balconies with bursts of color. In one corner, nestled between potted palms, a carved stone fountain bubbled quietly. Overhead, strands of soft lighting ribboned across the courtyard, casting a warm, romantic glow upon the flagstone floor. The sweet, exotic scent of orchids and hibiscus perfumed the balmy evening air with a touch of magic.

Their host guided them to a table for two by the fountain, draped in crisp white linen and set with sparkling crystal glasses.

Della hesitated, wondering why he'd directed them to such an intimate table.

"There must be some mistake," Logan said, echoing her thoughts. "There are four in the Williams party."

"Mr. Williams called a few minutes ago and changed his reservation to tomorrow evening," the man replied smoothly. "This table is correct." He placed the menus on the tabletop and pulled Della's chair out, then gently pushed it in for her as she sat. In one deft move, he snatched the napkin off the table and spread it across her lap. Then he did the same for Logan. With a polite bow, he added, "Enjoy your dinner."

"Well," Logan said with a wry smirk as he opened his menu. "It looks like *Mr. Williams* decided we were cramping his style."

Della fished her phone from her purse and quickly texted Lainey.

Where r u?

Lainey promptly texted back. *Giving you and Logan some space. Enjoy dinner!*

Della looked up from her phone. "I think Lainey and Tarone planned it this way on purpose. They want us to dine alone."

Logan laughed. "Knowing Williams, he changed his reservations without telling me because *he* wanted to dine alone with his new girlfriend."

After a serving assistant filled their water glasses, their waiter appeared at their table, a short, freckled young lady with platinum hair and ruby-red lips, wearing a white shirt and black slacks. "Would you like to start with a cocktail or perhaps some wine?"

Logan opened the wine menu. "Della, do you like red wine?" At her nod, he shut the menu and handed it to the waiter. "A bottle of Murphy-Goode Cabernet, please."

"So," he said as he sat back, "aside from all the drama today, how is everything with you? Did that coupon bring in new customers?"

"As you know, your sister came in yesterday," she said pointedly, deciding to cut to the chase. "Did she stop by your place to retrieve her earrings?"

His carefree smile vanished. "Yeah, but I was busy with a customer at the time, so I didn't get a chance to talk to her. What did she want?"

Della sat back and folded her hands on the table, keeping her tone casual. "A trim."

Logan's expression turned to stone. "I know Michelle. What did she *really* want?"

Just then, a server appeared with a paddle-shaped cutting board containing a small loaf of warm French bread, a serrated knife, and freshly whipped butter. The small interruption gave Della a moment to frame her words carefully.

"She said you were a great catch," Della began slowly, "but not the right one for me. I don't know why, but she seemed to think you and I were more than just friends. She informed me that your family has big plans for you and that I was not to get in your way."

Logan reached across the table, covering her hand with his. The affection in his strong fingers, intertwining with hers, made her heart flutter. "Don't pay any attention to her, okay? She doesn't know what she's talking about. My stepfather kicked me out of the house because I refused to come back to work for him. He's not backing down, and neither am I, so that's that. I'm officially a starving artist, but a very happy one at the moment." He smiled, his eyes shining as he lightened the mood. "I can't think of anywhere else I'd rather be tonight."

Della didn't have a chance to respond before their server returned with the wine and poured it into their glasses. As soon as she left, Logan raised his glass. "To our success."

They clinked glasses and sipped their wine.

"It's kind of funny," Della said with a soft laugh.

Logan swirled the dark liquid in his glass and took another sip. "What is?"

"Here we are, having dinner together, and yet, we don't know much about each other."

Logan picked up the knife and began slicing the bread. "All right then. You go first. Tell me everything I need to know about you in one minute."

Della laughed. "Okay, but you asked for it! I have one sibling—an older sister who is an IT executive by day. By night, she's an ambassador for the City of St. Paul. And get this—she wears a crown. She excels at everything she does and never misses an opportunity to rub it in my face. That's all I'm going to say about her."

She snatched up her wine glass, inhaling the rich notes of ripe blackberry, black cherry, and plum that drifted to her nose. "My mom is an elementary teacher, and my dad teaches economics at a state college. Just before I started kindergarten, they bought a new house plus a new car, and they still own both. My mom drives a newer SUV, but my dad proudly still drives the old Chevy. Everything is paid off, and they save money like pack rats. And they call me every day because they worry about me." She ended her speech with a sip of wine. "Your turn."

Logan smiled. "What is your sister's name?"

"Christina."

He handed her a thick, buttered slice of bread. "And your parents?"

"Rachel and Bill." She chomped on the bread, becoming a little annoyed. "I thought this was a one-minute intro, not twenty questions."

"I might meet them someday, so I need to know," he replied matter-of-factly.

His admission caught her off guard. Did he really like her enough to want to meet her family?

Logan hesitated, his gaze lingering on his wine glass. "So," he said, his voice softening, "what do you want to know about me?"

She leaned forward, challenging him with a mischievous smile. "If we were contestants on a game show, the category would be 'True Confessions.' The question would be, 'Who is Logan Chandler?' And the answer in sixty seconds is..."

He began to laugh. "I have a sister who is two years older than me, whom you've met, and an older brother, Jon. He's a CPA and a tax lawyer who works at my parents' firm along with Michelle. My parents built our house on the island before I was born because they wanted to keep their personal lives separate from the firm. My real dad died in a boating accident when I was seven, and a year later, my mom married Grant, who was the firm's senior tax lawyer at the time. Without my dad around, I was a brat growing up, and if it wasn't for Charles' steady hand guiding me, I probably would have kept right on being a major disappointment to my family." He let out a cynical laugh. "Oh, wait. I still am!"

Their server appeared out of nowhere, cutting into their reverie. "Would you like to order?"

"Yes," Logan said. "I'd like to order new parents, please!"

They burst out laughing and opened their menus.

The server stared at them in confusion, as if she didn't know what to make of the joke.

Settling down, they ordered their meals and spent the rest of the evening having a pleasant dinner, steering clear of personal issues. After dessert, Logan escorted her home.

As they stepped out into the warm, balmy night, the cloudless sky glittered with stars like scattered diamonds. The full moon cast a soft, silvery glow upon their faces. The steady, high-pitched chirping of cicadas serenaded them in a warm, rhythmic chorus.

"It's still early," Logan said as they approached her front door. "Would you like to take a stroll to the park? We could walk down to the waterfront as well."

"That sounds like fun," Della said with a yawn, still tipsy from consuming her half of the wine bottle, "but I need to get up early tomorrow to do some work around the salon. Why don't we take a walk another evening instead? Then we can take our time."

In the moonlight, she caught a flicker of disappointment crossing his face as his smile faded. "All right, but I'm going to hold you to that," he said, his voice dropping to a husky whisper. The tension in his tone made his response sound more like a vow than a promise. He closed the distance between them, sliding his strong arms around her waist, pulling her into his embrace.

For a heartbeat, she hesitated, uncertain if she was ready to take their friendship to the next level. As if sensing her reluctance, he loosened his grip and slipped one finger under her chin, gently tilting her face upward with a tenderness that made her heart skip a beat. Her resolve melted away, and she rose onto her toes, meeting him halfway. Her arms slid around his neck, holding on as though she could keep this moment suspended forever.

His lips brushed hers, tentatively at first, as if giving her one last chance to pull away. Instead, she leaned in, permitting him to deepen the kiss. He responded slowly and deliberately until the world around them blurred, leaving only the eager crush of his mouth and the wild thudding of her heart.

When the kiss ended, they reluctantly pulled apart. Logan's gaze softened as it lingered on her face, his voice barely above a whisper. "Ever since we met on the ferry, I've wondered what it would be like to kiss you." He paused, a gentle smile tugging at his lips. "Not just a passing thought—really wondering, but I didn't know how much I wanted it until now." His thumb brushed lightly over her knuckles. "Now that we're together, I don't want to wonder anymore."

As he kissed her again, the world seemed to hush around them. The only sound she heard was the quick thud of her heart as it leapt in her chest. His kiss was warm, unhurried, and full of feeling, like he'd been holding back for far too long. She melted into it, her hands finding the steady strength of his shoulders, her breath catching as a dozen emotions surged at once. When they finally parted, she didn't pull away. She leaned forward, resting her forehead against his, her eyes still closed, her heart still racing.

"Until next time," he murmured.

He unlocked the door for her and pushed it open, then lightly kissed her goodnight. "Sweet dreams. I'll see you tomorrow."

After Logan left, Della locked the door again, slipped off her shoes, and skipped up the back stairs to her apartment, still basking in the lingering glow of his kiss. His touch had felt so sincere, so real, yet a whisper of doubt echoed in the back of her mind. Was this the beginning of something meaningful, or had Logan simply become caught up in the magic of the moment?

She went into her bedroom and tossed her shoes into her small closet as her thoughts tumbled in a mixture of hope and hesitation. Could she trust him, or was she just a fleeting spark, powerless to ignite a flame? She had no idea.

Pushing all troubling thoughts from her mind, she spent leisurely twenty minutes soaking in her claw-footed tub, growing more relaxed and sleepier by the minute. Grabbing a towel, she stepped out of the tub and slid into a comfy pair of summer pajamas.

The night was warm, but her apartment was even warmer. She didn't have an air conditioner yet and had to settle for nature's way instead by opening all the windows to allow the cool breeze blowing off the sea to lower the temperature. The lights were next. Taking a deep breath, she slid into her soft bed and closed her eyes.

An odd creaking sound woke her. In her sleep-induced haze, it sounded as though someone had opened the wooden screen door downstairs, stretching the old, rusting spring to its limit. She lay still, listening. There it went again. Fully awake now, her mind focused on the unnatural sound coming through her kitchen window.

She sat up, groggily wondering if she should check it out. Her apartment was so tiny that it only took a couple of steps to reach the kitchen window. The creaking sound was clear now. Yes, someone definitely stood at the back door. The small alarm clock on her kitchen counter showed one o'clock in the morning in glowing white numerals.

She leaned in and pressed her head to the screen to see the person standing on her back stoop. "Logan? Is that you?"

The deafening silence that ensued sent her heart into a tailspin.

Someone was trying to break into the salon. And now they knew that *she knew*. She hurried back into the bedroom and grabbed her phone, pulling up Logan's number as fast as she could. He answered on the third ring.

"Yeah," he said in a slow, muffled tone.

"Logan, it's me, Della. I'm scared."

"Whaaa—what?" He paused, as though becoming fully awake. "What's the matter?"

"Someone is trying to break into the salon," she whispered. "Through the back door."

"H—hold on, okay? I'll call the cops. Stay on the line. I'll get right back to you."

Making a snap decision, she threw open the kitchen door and rushed down the stairs, her bare feet softly padding on the creaky wooden risers. "I can't stay here!" she whispered. "I'm coming to you!" She dashed through the salon, her heart racing faster than her feet. She unlocked the front door and burst onto the sidewalk. She ran toward Logan's gallery, shouting into the phone. "Logan? Logan!" The line sounded dead, but rather than try to call him back, she sprinted down the street, heading for his place. She'd run a block before he came back on the line.

"Della, the cops are on their way. Lock the apartment door and sit tight. I'll be right there."

"I can't," she cried breathlessly as she stubbed her toe on the cement pavement and winced in pain. "I'm almost at the gallery right now. Come down and let me in. I'll be at the front door!"

Chapter Twelve

Logan rushed out of the building in his blue plaid pajama pants and a gray T-shirt, running straight into Della. By the time she'd reached the gallery, she was out of breath. Engulfing her in his arms, he cradled his hand on the back of her head, burying her face in his broad chest. "Della! I'm so glad you're safe, but you shouldn't have taken off. You would have been safer to lock yourself in your apartment until I got there. What if the intruder came after you and ran you down?"

"Oh, Logan, I was so scared," she cried as she sobbed into his chest. "I didn't see his face, but I wasn't sticking around to find out. I didn't think—I just bolted as fast as I could out the front door to get away."

He held her tighter, knowing he couldn't live with himself if anything happened to her.

Red and blue flashing lights turned onto Main Street, speeding toward the hair salon.

He pulled her from his arms. "The cops have arrived. We'd better get going." His gaze dropped to her bloody toe, then sped upward, halting abruptly. He swallowed hard. "Where are your shoes? And what are you wearing? Is that your underwear?"

Della froze, speechless at first. She stared down at her skimpy peach tank top with spaghetti straps reaching just above her navel and her mini-boxer shorts, looking as though she didn't understand the question at first. Her head jerked upward. "What? No, these are my pajamas. It's beastly hot in my apartment and I don't have a fan upstairs yet—"

"Don't worry about it," he said. Reaching over his shoulder to the nape of his neck, he grabbed the back of his T-shirt in his fist and jerked it over his head. He held it out to her. "Put this on."

Della slipped the T-shirt over her body and adjusted the shoulders. The shirt hung on her like a tent, but at least it covered her—

He let out a sigh of relief. Objective met.

She shot him an appreciative glance, but he was already moving and didn't have time to comment. They took off jogging toward the police car. Logan kept a brisk pace, holding on to the waistband of his pants to keep them from slipping lower.

When they reached the salon, they came face to face with Sheriff Hall. He stood next to his cruiser with his arms folded and his legs crossed at the ankle. His jaw dropped in slow motion as his gaze traveled in disbelief from Della's man-sized T-shirt to Logan's bare chest and plaid pants, which were barely covering his hips. He pulled off his hat and scratched his head. "You two…uh…having a fashion emergency?"

Della cleared her throat and smoothed her shirt, as though attempting to act like the outfit was perfectly normal. "I was just…you know…borrowing this. My apartment is sizzling hot and…" She glanced at Logan, looking flustered.

"Right," Sheriff Hall said quickly in his Caribbean accent, ending most of his sentences on an up-note. "You reported an intruder. When I got here, I found da front door wide open, but I checked inside and it's clear. My deputy checked around back and said it's clear there, too. Where did he try to break in?"

Della took the men into the salon and opened the back door. "I heard the spring on the back screen door making noise like this—" The ancient coil creaked loudly as she pulled open the door, stretching it. "See? It's so loud you can hear it through the upstairs window. I didn't see who it was, though. It's too dark back here."

"I'll start patrolling this area more often, especially da alley," the sheriff said. "From now on, I suggest you keep da back light on all night. It wouldn't hurt to put up a security camera, either."

"I plan to," Logan said. "After the windows were sprayed, Tarone and I ordered enough cameras for both businesses, but the brand we want is so popular that they're backordered. We're going to install them inside and at both entrances of the buildings. I'll sleep a lot better when Della's got good security."

Sheriff Hall frowned but didn't comment. He pulled out a notebook and began to jot down facts about the case. He looked at Della. "Do you have any enemies, miss?"

"No, I just moved to the island," Della said, sounding baffled. "I can't think of anyone who would want to do something like this…except…" She chewed on her lower lip. "Except maybe Vince Bernard."

Sheriff Hall angled his head as he wrote. "Bernard, huh? Right. I'll pay him a visit tomorrow. He's getting a stern warning to stay away from you or face the con-see-quences. Once you get those cameras up, we'll catch him if he tries it again. In da meantime, I'll check with da businesses along da alley to see if anyone saw or heard anything." He slapped his notebook shut and slipped it back into his pocket. "All right. Dat should do it." He bowed slightly, flashing a boyish grin. "I'll let you two get back to having fun."

Logan glanced at Della, then back at the sheriff. "Um…yessir. Thanks for answering my call so fast."

He waited until Sheriff Hall left the salon, then stood in the center of the room, checking out the best spots to place the security cameras. "We'll put one above the front door facing this way to cover the salon," he said, using his free hand to illustrate his idea, "and one in the back entryway facing the back door and the stairs."

Ignoring him, Della walked over to the sink and reached up, opening the cabinet door. She grabbed a bottle of Blackwell Jamaican Rum and two glasses.

Logan stopped what he was doing, staring at the rum bottle with curiosity. "Isn't this kind of late for a drink? Besides, I thought you only drank wine."

She placed the bottle and glasses on the counter. "It's Lainey's. Tarone gave it to her as a grand opening present. She told me I could help myself to it." She grabbed the bottle and twisted off the cap. "I'm celebrating Vince Bernard's arrest in advance. Want some?"

Logan looked away and began planning the security camera layout again. He had a mind to get on his computer as soon as he got back home and check on the status of his order. "I'd rather have a Coke."

Della opened a small refrigerator filled with water, soda, and juice. She grabbed the ice cube tray from the freezer and a can of soda, then fixed him a Coke. Then she poured a generous amount of rum into her glass with a splash of Coke for herself.

"If Vince Bernard thinks he's going to scare me into quitting just to get revenge, I've got news for him," she said stubbornly and held the glass to her lips. Gulping half of the liquid, her face turned crimson before she suddenly erupted into a fit of coughing. "He caught me by surprise tonight, but never again," she managed to say in between coughs. Grabbing the bottle, she added more booze to her glass.

"Hey, slow down there, tiger," Logan cautioned, pulling the glass from her hand before patting her back. "We don't have anything to celebrate yet. Besides, we don't have any proof."

She snatched the glass back, sloshing liquid over the back of her hand. "You *know* he did it. He said he was going to get even with you in front of everyone at Nigel's. Targeting me and Lainey is one way to get back at you and Tarone." She took another gulp, swallowing it down with a shudder. "He'd better not try to flaunt it in my face by coming here to get his hair cut," she said angrily. "I'll shave his head!" She suddenly broke into an uncontrollable giggle.

Tarone's red sports car screeched to a stop in front of the salon. Lainey jumped out and burst through the front door.

"Della!" Lainey cried. "Are you okay?"

"She's fine," Logan replied, surprised to see them. "How did you find out so quickly?"

Tarone led a dog on a leash as he followed Lainey into the room. "Duane told us as we were leaving Nigel's. He said he'd just left here and wanted to warn us about the attempted break-in."

Tarone glanced from Logan's bare chest to Della's T-shirt and moved close. "Hey, man," he murmured confidentially, "are we interrupting something?"

Logan nearly dropped his glass. "No, it's not what it looks like."

Tarone flashed a knowing smile. "Sure…"

Lainey picked up the bottle of rum and held it to the light. "Hey, it looks like you two are having quite a party on my booze. When I said to help yourself, I didn't mean drain the bottle!"

Della laughed. "Logan isn't drinking. Just me."

Lainey opened the cabinet and put the bottle away. "That's enough for you, girl. I think you're getting drunk."

Della placed the glass to her lips but barely got a sip before Lainey snatched it away. "Hey! You'd get drunk too if you had to sleep alone in this place tonight. It's turning out to be crime central!"

Lainey grabbed the leash from Tarone. "Not anymore," she announced with a proud smile. "Meet Zeus, our new guard dog. Want to pet him?" She crouched beside a stocky, medium-sized dog. His short, brindle coat stretched over so much solid muscle he looked like a fifty-pound ham. The dog's massive jaw was a beast in itself, stretching from one floppy ear to the other. He looked like he could chew through steel just to kill time.

The animal silently glanced up at Logan, staring at him as though daring him to make a wrong move. "I'll pass," he said cautiously, slowly stepping away.

"Oh, what a sweet dog!" Della exclaimed and sank to her knees on the floor to pet him. Zeus' smooth, thick tail began to swish, slapping against the cabinet with a loud thump, thump, his big brown eyes gazing at her adoringly as his wide, sticky tongue sloshed across her face. "What breed is he?"

Lainey rubbed one of Zeus' perky ears. "He's an American Pit Bull Terrier. Isn't he just the biggest baby you've ever seen? I got him in Miami at a rescue. The staff on the ferry had a fit when I brought him on board to bring him home!"

Della scratched him under the chin, cooing to him. "He's well-mannered. I have to say that for him," she said, slurring her words, "but if he's a big baby, how's he going to protect me?"

Lainey and Tarone began to laugh. Zeus looked up at them and began panting, his large tongue hanging out of his cavernous mouth.

"He loves women," Tarone stated matter-of-factly. "He's really protective of them, but not men. Especially strangers. He's liable to take someone's arm off if they try to break in here again."

Logan backed up farther. "What about all the strangers who'll be coming to the salon for hair appointments?"

"I've got a baby gate," Lainey said, pointing to the back of the salon. "We'll use it in the doorway so Zeus can move freely from the apartment to the back hallway while the salon is open." She kissed the dog on the top of the head. "He's just a big teddy bear."

Logan stared down at the dog, hoping the island cops would catch whoever was committing these crimes and stop him so the Jackhammer Jaw masquerading as a teddy bear wouldn't be needed.

Chapter Thirteen

"I'll take whoever is next in line," Della said, sweeping dark strands of hair from the floor with a small broom.

"My turn!" A middle-aged woman in a blue printed dress with short gray hair hustled across the room with the determination of a turtle crossing the highway. She plopped into the barber chair with a loud grunt and held up a small piece of paper. "Here's my discount coupon," she declared. "I want that haircut." She pointed to a large poster on the wall of a woman with a pixie haircut. The look was short and spiky. Effortlessly stylish. The low-maintenance aspect of this style made it popular because it required little fuss, except for an occasional trim and a dab of mousse to dress it up. Women had been coming in to get that cut since the day Della had tacked the poster to the wall.

"Thank you, ma'am," Della replied, exhaling a silent sigh of relief as she accepted the coupon and draped the salon cape around the woman's shoulders. Their business was starting to grow. The volume of walk-in customers increased every day, mostly due to the large network of friends of Lainey's mom and aunts.

News of the vandalism to the front of the building and the subsequent attempted break-in traveled across the island faster than the speed of sound, bringing a lot of curious customers to the salon. Both Della and Lainey were swamped with women who wanted their hair done, their nails done, or both. *Everybody* came looking for gossip.

Zeus immediately became the star attraction. He spent his day looking like a sphinx sitting behind the baby gate, watching the activity. He quickly learned that whining for attention would bring him petting and treats his way. Customers loved to baby him.

Late Wednesday morning, the members of Lainey's mom's Bible study group descended on the salon after their meeting, eager for haircuts and manicures and a look at the new hairstylist who had been seen holding hands at the Morganville Hotel with Logan Chandler.

Even Elsie Dubois shuffled through the door that afternoon for a trim. On the house, of course! By the next morning, members of the Island Women's Business League began trickling in, bringing homemade treats to share—and plenty of gossip.

One hot topic was the art fair at the LaBore Museum, the island's premier historic attraction. Once a slave plantation, it was now a beautifully restored landmark that served as a cultural center to the island. Only entries from island residents were eligible to enter the art fair, making the competition even fiercer.

Why didn't Logan tell me about this? Della wondered in disappointment as she cut and styled the hair of a young sculptor named Danica.

"I'm so excited about my entry in the art fair," Danica chattered excitedly as Della blew dry her long, dark hair. "But I'm nervous, too." She let out a tense sigh. "I just hope I make it through the first round of judging. Keep your fingers crossed for me! The coordinators are announcing the finalists this Friday!"

Della wondered if Logan had entered any of his paintings. "Do you by any chance recall seeing a painting by Logan Chandler? A watercolor, perhaps?"

Danica shook her head. "All of the entrants are anonymous until the awards ceremony next week."

Logan must not have entered the art fair, Della reasoned. Otherwise, why wouldn't he have mentioned it? She pushed the thought aside as Danica rattled on, but the thought wouldn't let her go. She needed to ask him about it to be sure.

On Thursday morning, a tall, willowy woman with cinnamon-toned skin stepped into the salon wearing a flowing maroon dress patterned with orchids and matching lipstick, carrying a large vase of fresh-cut flowers. Thick, spiraled curls of ebony hair bounced playfully around her neck and shoulders.

"Good morning," she announced in a rich Bahamian accent, her warm, generous smile brightening up the room. "On behalf of the Island Women's Business Association, I'd like to welcome you to Enchanted Island." Colorful bracelets adorning her long arms chimed softly as she offered Della the beautiful, fragrant flowers. "I'm Shakara Allain-LaMaur, the association president. I speak for the entire membership when I say that we wish you tremendous success." The words ending with an *r* sound were pronounced *ah*.

Shakara was everything Della had heard about her—and more. Strikingly beautiful, Shakara possessed an effortless grace that turned every head as she walked into the room. No wonder she'd been picked to represent the women of this island. Shakara's smile and genuine warmth had a way of making people feel seen, valued, and welcome.

"Thank you," Della replied, returning a smile as she graciously received the flowers. "I'm Della Delaney." She turned to Lainey. "Lainey and I are partners."

"Shakara!" Lainey exclaimed and rushed toward the woman, hugging her. "Thank you so much. Della and I were considering joining the association. How would we go about it?"

"Wonderful! Simply go to our website, fill out the form, and submit your dues," Shakara said. "Have you heard about the LaBore

Museum art fair?"

"Yes!" Lainey replied.

"A little," Della replied at the same time. "Since I'm new here, I hadn't heard about the event until recently."

"You and Lainey must come to the art fair!" Shakara exclaimed. "It's the first time the museum has held one, but it is already so popular that the Board plans to make it an annual event. Our business association is a major sponsor this year, and tomorrow evening, there is a special reception for donors. There is a limited number of tickets, so it's first-come, first-served, but as a member of the association, you'll also receive free admission to view the exhibition."

"Are we allowed to bring a guest?" Della asked, wondering if Logan wanted to attend with her. Perhaps he'd already viewed the exhibition. If so, why did he fail to mention that at dinner?

"Of course," Shakara replied enthusiastically. "Email Elsie Dubois with your information right away and ask if there are any tickets left."

"I'm on it now," Lainey said as she stood at the counter working on her laptop computer.

Shakara bid them goodbye and left the salon, promising to meet up with them again on Friday evening at the museum.

"Okay. One tap and we're in," Lainey said as she hit send on her computer. "I'll send Elsie an email letting her know that we've joined and that we'll be attending the event tomorrow evening. Shall I list Logan as your guest?"

"Um…yeah," Della said, hoping that Elsie had four tickets left. "But maybe we'd better wait on asking the guys until we actually hear from Elsie and can confirm that we have the tickets."

Later that day, after the salon had closed, Della and Lainey went upstairs to her apartment to feast on Chinese takeout. Zeus sat next to

Lainey's chair, whining for a piece of delicious chicken.

"This chicken lo mein is s-o-o-o good. I'm glad you talked me into getting takeout," Della said and stuffed her mouth with tasty noodles.

Lainey pulled the thin paper off her egg roll and began to cut it into sections, feeding one to Zeus. He swallowed it in one gulp. "Everything at House of Woo is fantastic, but my favorite will always be kung pao chicken. I love spicy food." She opened a packet of duck sauce and poured it into a small bowl, then went still. "Did you hear that? I could swear I heard the door close. Downstairs. It sounded like someone just came into the salon."

Della stopped eating and listened for a moment, then shrugged. "No. How would they get in without jingling the door chime?"

Zeus sat deadly still, his ears perked up, listening. The floor suddenly creaked, and he took off, growling. When he reached the main floor, he began barking.

"I don't know, but it might be someone looking to make an appointment." She jumped up. "I'll be right back." Her footsteps creaked on the wooden stairs. "Zeus! Come here!" Suddenly, she shrieked. "Della!"

Della flew down the stairs and found Lainey standing alone at the counter, reading a folded note. The front door stood open. Zeus sniffed about the room, as if still detecting someone's brief presence. "What is it?"

Lainey stared at the note with her lips pursed, then handed it to Della.

"*Two girls. One salon. One warning. Your days are numbered,*" Della read aloud. Her voice wavered with anger as she looked into Lainey's eyes. "Someone isn't just trying to scare us. They're threatening our lives!" She tossed the note onto the table. This wasn't some prank. This felt personal. "I don't know what kind of game Bernard thinks he's playing, but I've had it with his bullying."

Lainey's eyes narrowed, matching Della's rage. "Nobody is going to threaten us and get away with it." She folded her arms, glaring with indignation. "I'm going to fix this idiot. I'm going to make Bernard—or whoever did this—regret the day he decided to pick on me. You in, girl?"

"Yeah," Della spouted, liking Lainey's spunk. "But let's keep this to ourselves, okay? The more Logan and Tarone know about our plan, the more likely *they* will interfere."

Lainey nodded quickly. "Deal. Let's go!"

They smacked their palms together in a loud, satisfying high-five and began planning their revenge.

Chapter Fourteen

Logan stood in the main area of his gallery, a spacious, well-lit room with white walls and ceilings, hanging a large watercolor on the wall, when his cellphone rang. He picked it up and checked the number. He couldn't tell if the call came from a telemarketer or if someone had decided to prank him. The phone rang two more times before he realized it might be one of the galleries he'd approached in Miami. He answered it just before the call went to voicemail.

"Main Street Gallery, Logan Chandler speaking," he said apprehensively.

"Good morning, Mr. Chandler," a man replied with a Bahamian accent. His deep, melodious voice sounded familiar… "This is Hennrick Curry of the LaBore Museum. I'm calling with good news. Congratulations, your entry is a finalist in the first annual Enchanted Island Fine Arts Festival."

Logan stared at the floor, so shocked at first that he didn't know what to say. "Thank you. Thank you very much. I—I never expected this…"

Hennrick laughed. "You're the fourth person I've called so far, and everyone has said the same thing. The winners will be announced a week from tomorrow at the museum. Cocktail hour starts at six o'clock. Dinner at seven. Your invitation and special instructions will come by email next week. And—as much as you're tempted to tell your family and friends, remember that the entries must remain anonymous until the awards reception."

"Yeah…yeah sure," Logan replied, still so stunned by his good fortune that the words were difficult to come by. "All right. Thank you again. See you then."

He hung up the phone and went upstairs to his apartment to grab a beverage. What he really wanted was a cold beer to celebrate, but he didn't drink during business hours.

I'm a finalist…wow, he thought to himself as he selected a chilled bottle of Coke from the fridge. *Now what?*

He didn't have time to ponder the question. The bell chimed above the front door, signaling a visitor. He quickly ran downstairs to find Charles slowly walking through the room, studying every painting he had on display.

"Did you get da call?" Charles asked as he stopped in front of Logan.

"Yeah, how did you know?"

Charles chuckled. "C'mon, son. Did you really think you wouldn't make da final round?"

Logan shrugged as he twisted the cap off his bottle. "I guess I didn't know what to think. I've never done this before."

"You're going to take first place," Charles said confidently as he laid a steady hand on Logan's shoulder. "Trust me. I've got faith in your talent." He shoved his hands into his pants pockets, the soft jingle of loose change punctuating his words. "The awards ceremony is next weekend. You planning to take dat cute little hairstylist you've been seeing?"

Logan rubbed the back of his neck, suddenly realizing he hadn't spoken to Della about the art fair. He never expected to become a finalist, so the thought of talking to her about the event hadn't crossed his mind. Hopefully, she hadn't made other plans. "Yeah, if she wants to go."

Charles raised one brow. "I heard from a friend that Barb and Grant are sponsoring a table for six people. If you want to sit with your parents, you need to speak up before they fill da seats with their friends." When Logan didn't respond, he said, "Don't you think you should get on that?"

"Della is probably busy with appointments this morning," Logan said, checking his watch. "I hate to interrupt her when she's working. I'll give her a call at lunchtime. Then I'll call Mom."

With a wry chuckle, Charles shook his head. "If it was me, I'd hustle down to her shop right now and ask her out before someone else does, but what do I know?" He pointed toward Logan's cast. "How's your wrist coming along?"

Logan stared at his cast, turning his palm upward. "I'm getting used to it, but it's difficult to do anything with my hand right now. I've tried practicing with a brush. It got uncomfortable right away, so for the heck of it, I tried switching to my left hand. It's a little awkward, but not impossible. I've decided I might as well use this time to train my non-dominant hand to paint."

Charles nodded with approval. "Drawing is mastered first with your eyes and your heart, not your hand. Embrace your discomfort and keep at it. You'll get there." He glanced around the gallery, surveying Logan's other paintings, but then paused, offering a sincere smile. "Congratulations, Logan. On all of this. You've made me proud."

"Thank you. That means a lot to me." His voice thickened with emotion as a rush of gratitude filled his heart. He said goodbye to Charles, wondering what to do about the awards dinner and ceremony as the weight of the situation settled on him. Of course, he wanted to be with Della, but the awards ceremony itself meant nothing to him unless

Charles could be there too. Charles deserved to have a seat at his parents' private table, but the likelihood of that was slim to none. No way would they invite an employee to join them. Still, he had to try.

He picked up his cellphone and called his mother at her office in Miami. It surprised him when she answered her cell phone in the office. Barb had a strict rule about no personal phone use during office hours.

"Logan, is there a problem?" The briskness of her business tone indicated that she had a busy schedule and didn't have much time to talk.

"No," he answered, though he knew she'd see it differently once she heard his request. "I've decided to attend the awards ceremony at the museum next weekend."

"Oh, that's wonderful, dear." Barb's voice lifted with cheer. "Michelle is attending. It'll be nice to have the family together for the evening."

"Does that mean Jon will be there, too?"

Barb hesitated. "I'm not sure. He hasn't gotten back to me yet."

Logan knew his older brother like a book. If Jon hadn't committed to the invitation by now, he wasn't coming. If he *had* agreed to attend, Logan would have talked him out of it anyway because he needed that extra chair. He drew in a deep breath. "I'm bringing a date."

"Michelle is attending alone, but if you're bringing someone, that leaves only one other seat," she said, her voice curt with disappointment. "We were planning to invite the Robinsons to join us."

"I want Charles to fill the last chair."

"Logan, that's out of the question," she snapped. "He's not affiliated with the museum." She hesitated. "Besides, he's our *gardener.*"

He'd expected excuses, but inferring that Charles' presence as a lowly *employee* would embarrass his parents in front of their peers angered him. "He's the reason I became an artist. He taught me everything I know. I want him at our table."

"It would be awkward, Logan. Inappropriate."

"Mom, please. It's important to me. I'm a finalist in the competition."

His announcement was met with an awkward silence as though Barb had never expected to hear those words from her son.

"That's why I want Charles to be there. He deserves this honor as much as I do."

"Congratulations, Logan," she replied softly. "This is such a surprise, but I'm very happy for you. As for Charles…I don't know what to say."

"It's easy, Mom. Just say yes."

I'll speak to Grant," she countered with an exasperated sigh, "but I can't promise anything."

After reminding her not to mention his finalist status to anyone, Logan ended the call more determined than ever. One way or another, Charles would be at that dinner.

Logan strolled over to the Island Glow Hair Salon right at noon. On Enchanted Island, every small business except for restaurants closed from noon to one o'clock every day. He was counting on that, hoping to find Della alone so they could talk privately.

"Hey, there," he said to her as he entered the brightly lit salon. Della stood sweeping hair clippings scattered across the floor. A white shop coat swished around her knees as she moved in rhythm to the Caribbean music playing in the background. A tall pedestal fan circulated the air throughout the room. To Logan's relief, Zeus lay curled up on his bed *behind* the gate, dozing peacefully. "Wanna get some lunch? Or do you have plans with Lainey?"

Della dropped the broom and rushed toward him, sliding her arms around his neck. "Lainey's having lunch with Tarone at the Amaryllis Resort. She's already gone."

"Then that leaves just you and me," he said, circling his arms around her waist. "How about we have lunch at the Morganville Hotel?"

"I'm more in the mood for Chinese," she said as she kissed him lightly. "It's such a nice day, let's get takeout at House of Woo and eat in the park. But I need to let the dog out to pee first. Okay?"

They picked up their food and found a shady spot at a picnic table in the park. While they ate, Logan brought up the idea that had been pressing on his mind. "The awards ceremony for the art fair at the museum is next Friday night." He leaned close and gazed into her eyes. "My parents are sponsoring a table for my family. Would you like to attend with me?"

"The awards banquet? Oh, my gosh, yes! I'd love to!" She paused, her chopsticks waving mid-air. She looked oddly relieved, as though she had been waiting for him to ask her that very question. "Now it's my turn. How would you like to accompany me to a private reception at the museum tonight?"

"Seriously?" Her offer surprised him so much that he nearly dropped a piece of sweet and sour pork. He had no idea she was such a fan of art. "Sure! How did you get tickets?"

"Lainey and I joined the women's business association today, and they're a major sponsor," she explained. "The museum is holding a private reception for the sponsors tonight. We just got confirmation from Elsie DuBois as we were closing for lunch that tickets were still available, so we each asked for two. It starts at seven o'clock. Lainey is bringing Tarone."

"Great. I'll pick you up at six-thirty," Logan said softly. "I'm looking forward to it." Showing her around the art exhibition filled him with quiet joy, but beneath his relaxed manner, a familiar knot twisted his gut. He still hadn't told her about the painting or the storm that it might stir up with his family. For now, though, he savored the moment, knowing it might be the last bit of calm before everything began to unravel.

The LaBore Museum, a majestic yellow plantation house with white gingerbread trim, sat high upon a hill on the south side of the island, surrounded by ten square miles of forests, beaches, and natural caves.

Twilight stretched along the Caribbean horizon, splashing the sky with soft crimson hues as Logan's car traveled along a winding gravel road through dense forest to a large parking lot down the hill from the museum. Once there, a lighted stairway guided them past the carriage house and outbuildings to the mansion.

The grand colonial house rose from the lawn like something out of a forgotten romance. Its soft yellow exterior glowed beneath the sway of palm trees, while two sweeping staircases curved down from the porch like open arms, meeting in the center, just above a winding path of weathered stones. White gingerbread trim traced every edge of the structure while slender columns framed the upper and lower verandas between tall arched windows. A pair of liveried doormen stood on each side of the front doors, welcoming them.

As Logan escorted Della to the entrance, he checked his phone. "I texted Tarone to let him know we're here." Before he got the words out, his phone pinged. Tarone had texted back to let him know that he and Lainey were waiting for them in the courtyard.

"Everything about this place feels suspended in time, like a secret tucked away at the edge of the island," Della said dreamily as Logan led her into a wide interior courtyard in the center of the building. The red brick flooring evoked a sense of days gone by, and the Tuscan stone columns rose elegantly around them. One story above, a decorative wrought iron railing framed the entire perimeter of the second-floor balcony. Twilight shone through the "lunette" or half-moon-shaped windows set above the doorways lining the balcony.

Lainey and Tarone sat at a table draped with a crisp white cloth, sipping Cokes and nibbling on cheese and crackers from the buffet spread along the back wall. They stood as Logan and Della approached.

"Let's tour the exhibit," Tarone suggested.

"Yeah," Lainey chimed in. "I want to see the painting everybody's talking about. My mamma says all the buzz is about exhibit number two-hundred forty-three."

Logan swallowed hard and looked away, pretending to check the time on his watch. Exhibit #243 *was his*. What did Lainey mean by *all the buzz*? Who was talking about the painting, and what were they saying? Charles hadn't said a word to him about it, but if people were talking, Charles would know. He needed to ask the man.

Back at the gallery, he'd kept quiet about entering the art fair, changing the subject whenever customers mentioned it. He didn't want anyone to think that owning an art gallery gave him an advantage or suspect that he'd entered the most controversial painting in the competition. Once the winners were announced and he lost, he'd get the painting back and bury it in the back closet where it belonged.

"Let's start at the carriage house," Logan offered, hoping to steer Della away from potential controversy. "The sculptures and pottery items are on display there."

Lainey pointed toward the wrought iron railing along the balcony of the second floor. "The hallway upstairs is filled with photography and paintings. Tarone wants to check it out."

"Okay, we'll meet you back here in an hour," Logan said to them and walked to the carriage house with Della on his arm. He took his time examining every sculpture and piece of pottery in the place, pointing out his favorite pieces to Della.

"Wow," she exclaimed. "Some of these pieces are *really* good. Would you ever consider selling any of them in your gallery?"

"Absolutely," Logan replied enthusiastically. "Tarone has purchased partitions that we can use as floating walls, meaning we can move them around and position them any way we want, so we'll have more room to display items." He paused in front of a statue of a child kneeling in prayer. "I really like this one."

He stepped toward another large sculpture. "After the winners are announced, there might be other art dealers interested in some of these pieces," he said, "but I hope I can secure commitments for a few of my favorites to sell on commission at the gallery. Tarone and I think it's important to showcase the work of other local artists alongside ours."

"Ooooh, I love this one," Della exclaimed, walking toward a tall, slender ceramic statue of a black speckled cat.

Logan slid his arm around her shoulders and pulled her close. "If it's for sale after the exhibition, I'll get it for you," he murmured in her ear. "I think it would look perfect in your salon."

She hugged him, then glanced at the cast on his wrist. "Logan, that is so sweet of you, but can you afford it? You're going to be out of work for at least several more weeks."

laughed. "Maybe I don't have to pay money for it. What if I secure a trade instead? One of my paintings in exchange for this cat. Artists and crafters do that all the time."

"Thank you," she whispered, pressing a soft kiss to his lips. "Whenever I look at it, I'll think about you."

"I think about you all the time." He gazed into her eyes, his voice low and full of feeling.

The words hung between them, charged and tender, as if they'd stepped into a world made only for two.

Della's phone buzzed, interrupting the moment. "It's Lainey. I think we've been here too long." She answered the phone, and after a brief conversation, she hung up. "They ran into Shakara and Pete and got sidetracked. They haven't started looking at the exhibits yet. Lainey wants us to hurry up so we can view them together. She has some exciting news."

They made their way back to the mansion and went into the courtyard. Lainey waved to them from the upper balcony. Logan and Della climbed the stairs to the second floor, where a display of paintings and photography filled the open hallway.

Lainey glowed with excitement as they approached her. "Pete and Shakara invited us to be their guests at the awards ceremony!" she announced with a squeal. "The Morganville Hotel is sponsoring a table."

Della treated her to a hug. "That's great news. We can plan our outfits together!"

After that, Logan and Della wandered along the balcony, viewing the exhibits.

"There's a lot of talent here," she murmured as she gazed at the paintings on display, "but none of these compares to yours." She drifted toward a large brown-and-white oil painting of a historic scene. "Except this one…" She stared at it in astonishment. "Wow. This is fantastic." A wry smile tugged at her lips. "Gee, if I didn't know any better, I would have mistaken *you* for the artist—"

Logan slipped his arm in hers and steered her away from the painting. "You know what? I'm thirsty. Let's share a Coke and a plate of hors d'oeuvres before they're all gone."

She gave him a puzzled look. "What's the matter? Did I say something wrong?"

"No," he replied in a rush with an embarrassed laugh as he guided her toward the stairs and as far away from his painting as possible. "Why do you think that?"

At the top of the stairs, she pulled back. "The moment I tried to talk about that painting—number two forty-three, you cut me off and changed the subject. Why? What's wrong? Do you have a problem with it?"

He winced internally, knowing he'd handled it all wrong. He hadn't meant to upset her, but his actions had nothing to do with her finding out that he'd created the painting. Rather, his growing unease stemmed from the colossal mess his family's disapproval could create. He never expected to become a finalist, and now, with his controversial painting in the spotlight, the stakes felt even higher.

Family dynamics were complicated, especially his. The last thing he wanted was to expose Della to his family politics, especially when things had the potential to get heated. He couldn't allow his issues with them to sabotage something with Della that felt so right before it even had a chance to grow. Whatever happened next with them would need to be handled with care.

But for now, he needed to level with her. Della's trust in him was all that mattered.

"Let's get out of here," he began in a low voice. "There's something I need to tell you."

Chapter Fifteen

On Friday, the day of the awards ceremony, Della twirled gracefully in front of the mirror, taking in the full effect of her evening ensemble. Lainey's aunt had done a wonderful job of altering the gorgeous black dress that she'd purchased from an island thrift shop. Long and sleek, the strapless crepe gown draped naturally over her body, fitting her like a glove.

She checked the kitchen clock. Logan was due to arrive in five minutes. Grabbing her small black clutch and a lace shawl, she slipped on her black pumps and went downstairs to wait for him.

Zeus had gone to Lainey's house to spend the evening with her family. Della didn't like leaving him for hours without a potty break or someone to keep him company.

The bell chimed above the front door just as she arrived at the bottom of the stairs. Logan stepped into the salon wearing a black tuxedo and carrying a white plastic bag. The moment his eyes met hers, a look of wonder crossed his face. "You look amazing," he said softly, crossing the room to kiss her.

"I'm excited for tonight," she whispered as she slid her palms under the lapels of his jacket. "I just know you're going to win."

"Before we go, I have something for you," he said, reaching into the bag. He pulled out a clear plastic box containing an orchid corsage. "A beautiful dress needs a beautiful flower." Carefully, he pinned the delicate orchid on her.

Then he pulled out a long black velvet box and held it out to her. "This is also for you. Open it," he said, his voice merry with anticipation.

She lifted the lid to find a necklace and earring set made from clear sea glass, delicately encased in gold wire wrap. Her breath caught in her throat. "Oh, my gosh, Logan, it's beautiful."

"It's a one-of-a-kind set by Shakara Allain-LaMaur," he said softly. "The moment I saw it in the gift shop at The Amaryllis Hotel, I knew it was meant for you."

He lifted the necklace from the box, the sparkly gold chain and wire wrapping catching the light. "May I help you put it on?"

His long fingers deftly brushed her sensitive skin as he swept her hair aside, sending a tremor down her spine. He fastened the clasp, then pressed a soft kiss into the curve of her neck. "There," he murmured. "Do you like it?"

She turned to the large mirror on the wall again, her eyes glistening from this extravagant and unexpected gift. The effect was striking, a perfect finishing touch to her black-tie look. She turned, her voice catching in her throat. "I love it," she said, her voice barely above a whisper. "No one's ever given me anything so thoughtful."

"Maybe that's because I think about you all the time," he murmured. "I can't wait to show you off tonight at dinner. And at the party my parents are having after the awards ceremony. It's just for the museum board members, the winners, and art fair organizers. It'll give you a chance to get to know them better."

She smiled and slipped her arm in his. "I can't wait."

Della and Logan joined Lainey and Tarone at the cocktail party preceding the dinner. The museum staff had erected a huge white tent behind the building for the formal dinner and awards ceremony, but cocktail hour began in the inner courtyard of the museum.

"Della, you look fabulous in that dress," Lainey exclaimed as she greeted Della with a hug.

"I owe it all to your Aunt Celia," Della replied with a laugh. "She did a terrific job making me look good."

Della stood back, admiring Lainey's gold dress and sparkling jewelry. Tonight, she had wrapped her long braids into a round chignon at the nape of her neck. Diamonds adorned her ears and neck, glittering against her creamy Bahamian skin. "You look awesome, too."

"Hey, is that one of Shakara's creations?" Lainey asked, examining Della's pendant. Her smile quickly turned to a frown of disappointment. "So, you went shopping without me?"

"No way! I'd never do that." Horrified, Della shook her head. "It's a gift from Logan. He bought it at a fancy shop in the Amaryllis Hotel."

"Oh, my gosh, Della, it's beautiful…"

From the corner of her eye, Della noticed a small group of women watching them. "Lainey," she said, slightly nodding in their direction. "Who are those ladies over in the corner? I think they're talking about us."

Lainey tilted her head just enough to sneak a glance. "Oh," she remarked, her voice taking on a pessimistic tone, "that's—"

"Excuse me," Logan interrupted as he gently slipped his arm around Della's shoulders. "My parents are here, Della, and I'd like you to meet them."

He led her to a small cluster of elegantly dressed guests. The men wore tuxedos with effortless ease. The women shimmered in black designer gowns decked out with glittering jewels. The same women, she noted, who she'd caught staring at her and Lainey. They carried themselves with confidence that came only from old money and unshakable social standing.

"I wouldn't worry about it. He's probably not serious…" one of the women said softly as the group whispered among themselves. The conversation halted the moment Logan approached them with Della on his arm.

"Mom, I'd like you to meet Della Delaney," he said proudly, addressing a short, petite woman with a sleek, silver-blonde bob and hazel eyes that mirrored his. "Della, meet my mother, Barb Montclair." Though Logan's expression remained composed, Della sensed his unease. Why did this introduction feel more like a challenge than a welcome?

Barb's gaze swept over Della with a single, superior glance—poised, polite, and unmistakably appraising. "It's nice to meet you, Della," she said in a crisp, clear tone. "Aren't you one of the merchants on Main Street who received a grant?" The cool, casually dismissive way in which she phrased the question made the grant sound more like an embarrassing handout than a legitimate opportunity.

Della's spine stiffened instinctively. She wasn't ashamed of the grant or the tenacity it took to earn it. She'd fought hard for her place on Main Street and had no intention of shrinking beneath Barb Montclair's polished condescension. "Yes, I am," Della replied with a calm expression and a touch of pride in her voice. "I own the Island Glow Hair Salon."

"Where are you from?" one of the women asked curiously.

"I grew up in Minnesota," Della replied. To her surprise, her answer was met with a few muffled snickers.

"Isn't that part of Canada?" Barb asked, arching one brow.

Della blinked, letting her gaze settle on the women. They weren't being politely curious. They were mocking her. "Living on an island, I guess you probably wouldn't know that Minnesota is the thirty-second state in the union," she replied tartly. Obviously, these ladies were used to holding the upper hand in every conversation, but not this time.

"I can understand why you moved here," another woman said with a breezy laugh. "It's so cold up there!"

Della suppressed the urge to roll her eyes, realizing that she didn't want to play this game any longer. Besides, Logan was urging her to join him with the men. "Only in the winter. The rest of the year, the ten thousand lakes that cover my state are beautiful. If you'll excuse me, ladies…"

Logan slipped his arm around her as soon as she joined him, guiding her into his circle of gray-haired men. "Della, this is my stepfather, Grant Montclair."

She extended her hand. "Hello, Grant. It's nice to meet you."

Grant barely glanced at her. The tall, gray-haired man with handsome patrician features extended his hand almost as an afterthought, his grip brief and cool. "Nice to meet you, too. Enjoy your evening." Without waiting for a reply, he turned back to the man beside him to resume their conversation, as if he never expected to see her again.

Della stood still for a beat, the smile on her face tightening. So, this was the man who helped shape Logan's world—aloof, polished, and used to deciding who mattered in a room.

Drowning in a sea of strangers dressed in confidence and couture, she scanned the room, hoping to find her only friend, but Lainey and Tarone had vanished. "Excuse me, gentlemen." She took a deep breath and turned away from the group, intending to slip away and find Lainey. And calm her nerves.

"Della—wait."

Logan's voice stopped her before she made it to the edge of the room.

"I'm sorry for what happened back there. I knew this wouldn't be easy," he said, sounding frustrated. "My parents aren't exactly...warm. But they need to accept you."

"I didn't come here to beg for their approval," she said stubbornly. "But I also didn't expect to be treated like I was beneath notice. If you met *my* parents, they'd probably bombard you with twenty nosy questions, but they would be sincere about it. They'd want to get to know you for my sake. They're not perfect, but they do care."

"I'm sorry. I should've prepared you better." He paused, his voice dropping. "You deserve better than that." He took her hand and showered her with a smile that melted her heart. "It's a beautiful night for many reasons, but none as important as being here with you. Come on," he said, tugging her hand. "Let's get some air."

Laughter and music from the plantation house faded behind them as Della stepped carefully along a narrow path, clutching Logan's hand tightly for support until they reached the edge of the high bluff, where the world seemed to fall away into a velvet sea of stars. It was warm and peaceful here. The perfect place for just the two of them.

Below, the vast Caribbean stretched to the horizon, ink-dark and shimmering beneath the moonlight. Waves rolled in rhythmically, their foamy crests catching bits of silver as they broke against the rocks far below. The salty breeze rose from the ocean, cool and damp, carrying with it the mingled scents of brine and tropical flowers.

Down the cliffside, clusters of resort lights winked like scattered jewels along the curve of the shoreline, but up here, it felt like they were the only two people in the world.

She leaned into Logan, sliding her arms around his neck as he gently pulled her into his arms.

"I'm glad we took this time away," he said softly, his voice low and close. "I could tell you were getting upset." He pulled her closer. "Don't take it personally. It's just the way they are."

"You're not like them," Della said, seeing the contrast now more than ever. "Not at all."

"People tell me that I'm a lot like my father," Logan replied. "He moved us to this island to build a beautiful house surrounded by natural beauty. I remember how much he loved working in his garden. He wasn't the driving force behind the family business. My mother was and still is."

"And she wants you to fall in line like a good little soldier," Della said, ending the sentence for him. "She wants to control you like she runs her business."

He sighed. "Crunching numbers, making money. That's what it's all about for her and Grant. Never mind about them, okay? This evening is for us to celebrate—together—whether I win or not. I just want to be here with you."

He kissed her tenderly as though trying to console her. "I don't always know how to say what I'm feeling," Logan said, his voice softer now, as though admitting it more to himself than to her. "But you're in my thoughts—and my heart—all the time. I want you to know that."

"I never get tired of hearing it, Logan," she said softly, "but why me? I'm just a girl from Minnesota. What do I have that other women don't?"

He laughed. "You're fun, adventurous, and you don't care what anyone else thinks." Sliding his hand along the curve of her neck, he tilted her face forward and kissed her. "I don't know any girl who'd sprint down Main Street in the middle of the night in her pajamas to get away from an intruder. That was pretty brave if you ask me."

She placed her hands on his chest, feeling the cadence of his heart beneath her palms. It matched the tempo of her own, almost as if they'd both been waiting for this moment. "Knowing you were waiting for me at the gallery gave me the courage," she said, sounding calmer than she felt. But she meant it. She'd sensed the depth of his feelings for her even before he'd spoken them aloud. It showed in the caring way he looked at her, and in the attentive way he listened, even when she wasn't sure what she was trying to say.

The kiss came slowly, like neither of them needed to rush. Her arms tangled around his neck, while his arms encircled her waist. She leaned into him fully, letting herself believe that maybe this wasn't temporary or fragile.

The moonlight bathed the night in silver, softening the edges of their faces. As if even the night itself knew something had shifted— something delicate and important. Something worth holding on to.

And Della, for the first time in a long while, let herself believe it was okay to feel it.

Chapter Sixteen

With fingers entwined, Logan led Della back to the mansion. As they neared the dual staircase, a commotion at the front entrance caught his attention. The loud, insistent voice sounded familiar. Someone was being denied entrance into the event.

This better not be about Charles, he thought, becoming upset. *I told Mom to put his name on the guest list, whether Grant liked it or not.* The mere thought of Charles being turned away made his palms sweat and his temper flare.

Still gripping Della's hand, he hurried up the staircase to see who was so mightily upset about not getting into the event that his voice carried through the night. To Logan's surprise, it wasn't Charles. It was Vince Bernard.

"What's the problem here?" Logan asked as he and Della reached the check-in podium.

Vince spun around in a black suit and tie, his face flaming with disappointment and humiliation. "This lady says my ticket is no good."

"This is an exclusive event for the finalists, patrons, and pre-registered guests," the gray-haired woman standing behind the podium stated firmly. "Tickets are non-transferable."

Vince shoved the printed invitation in her face. "Kirk Stroebel is my boss! He owns Hideaway Cove Resort. He reserved a table for his managers, but he can't make it tonight, so he gave *me* his ticket to come in his place. Why is that so hard to understand?"

Logan had no idea why Vince, who'd probably never picked up an artist's brush or piece of modeling clay in his life, would want to attend an art event, but denying his entry simply because his name wasn't on the ticket didn't seem right. To him, it seemed downright snobby.

"C'mon, Mrs. Bennet," Logan said, stepping forward. "Give the guy a break. His boss is a major patron. If Mr. Stroebel decided to provide one of his employees with an opportunity to attend the museum's event of the year, then you should honor it."

She glanced at his dark suit and tie. "He's not wearing the proper attire. This is a formal event."

Logan glanced at Vince's clothes, guessing that the last time he wore this outfit was to a funeral. Regardless, the clothes were clean, and they looked new. "So what? He looks fine to me. Give the guy a break, would you?"

Mrs. Bennet pursed her lips, clearly unimpressed. "Rules are rules, Mr. Chandler."

"Then maybe it's time to make an exception," Logan replied, his voice calm but firm. "I'll vouch for him. He's with me."

Mrs. Bennett let out a loud, exasperated sigh. "Very well," she said, waving a hand dismissively. "Since you're a finalist, I'll do it for you."

And because my parents are top donors, he thought wryly. Sometimes money had its advantages. Being a finalist didn't hurt, either. At least, for tonight.

"Thanks, Logan," Vince offered sincerely, even though his face registered disbelief that Logan would go to bat for him. "I don't understand why you're helping me, but I appreciate it. Really, I do." He pointed at the special nametag on Logan's lapel. "So, you're a finalist, huh? That's great. Good luck."

"Thanks, I probably need it!" Logan replied with a chuckle, masking his surprise. In all the years he'd known Vince Bernard, the guy had never once said anything positive to him, much less something that could be considered *encouraging*. Maybe this was a start.

Logan almost laughed out loud in astonishment at the thought. Could this be the end of their lifelong rivalry? Not that either of them could remember exactly how it began—just years of tension, arguments, and fistfights stretching back to middle school.

"Say," Logan added, seizing the moment, "do you still do handyman work on the side?"

"Yeah, sure. Why?" Vince asked, falling into step with Logan and Della as they walked toward the inner courtyard.

"Tarone and I need help installing some new lighting in our gallery and assembling some movable divider panels. Being a maintenance man for a big resort, you must be pretty good at stuff like that. You interested?"

Vince's expression lit up at the suggestion. "Sure, give me a call," he said, flashing a grin. "I'll give ya a good deal."

"We're expecting the materials next week. I'll let you know when we're ready."

Vince paused. "I heard about the problems you guys have been having downtown with vandalism and an attempted break-in." He pointed his thumb at his chest, his eyes widening with indignation. "Sheriff Hall accused *me* of being the guy behind it, but I had nothing to do with it." He raised his palms in a peacemaking gesture. "I swear, Della! I don't know who's behind it, but if I hear anything, I'll let you know."

"Thanks," Logan replied sincerely.

They shook hands briefly before Vince left them, and they headed toward their respective tables. His claim of innocence seemed genuine. Working in a large resort gave Vince access to a lot of gossip, and Logan hoped that if Vince did come across some valuable information that he'd relay it to him.

In the meantime, having someone with Bernard's skills to call on when they needed help would come in handy, and he hoped that other merchants would hire him after seeing the work Vince did for him and Tarone.

Why am I helping this guy? Logan wondered, surprised by his change of attitude. *Because,* he thought determinedly, *I want to end this feud between us.* He stared down at the cast on his wrist and realized he had no one to blame but himself for his predicament. *I want to stop being angry.*

Vince had seen the cast on Logan's hand but didn't mention it. Perhaps he felt guilty for starting trouble. Perhaps he just wanted to move on and stop fighting, too.

Barb came barreling out of nowhere, looking frazzled. Her heels clicked sharply against the tile as she waved both arms. "Logan! Where have you been? Everyone's already seated in the marquee out back. Hurry!"

"Is Charles there too?" he asked quickly.

She gave a dismissive shrug, already half-turned away. "I have no idea. You're the only one who concerns me right now."

"Thanks for noticing me," Della whispered under her breath, her tone dry.

Logan tightened his grip on her hand and leaned in close. "Don't worry," he murmured encouragingly. "When we walk into the marquee, everyone's going to notice I'm here with the most beautiful woman in the room."

That earned him a soft, appreciative smile.

Behind the mansion, a sprawling white marquee dominated the back lawn. Its high-peaked ceiling soared over the round tables inside, glowing with the warmth of hundreds of suspended white lights. Plumeria in shades of fuchsia, mango, yellow, and blush filled low centerpieces on each round table, while flickering candles added a golden shimmer to polished silverware and china plates and cups embellished with the LaBore family crest. The air smelled faintly of jasmine and fresh-cut grass.

At the front of the tent, a dais stood ready for the evening's speakers. A sleek podium rested beneath soft uplighting, framed by bouquets of red and yellow canna lilies and a backdrop of fabric drapes in pale ivory.

Logan led Della down the central aisle between tables, drawing a few curious glances. His family's table was near the front in the area reserved for top-tier patrons. The rest of his family was already seated. Barb didn't look up, preoccupied with adjusting her napkin. Grant suddenly needed to check his watch. Michelle scrolled absently through her phone.

Logan pulled out a chair for Della, staring with concern at Charles' empty seat. He glanced around, his heart sinking with dread. If Charles didn't come, his evening would be a huge disappointment, making his accomplishment for naught.

And then, as if on cue, Charles entered the tent and walked straight toward the table wearing a smartly tailored tuxedo and patent leather shoes gleaming like obsidian. His dark skin contrasted against the brilliant white collar of his starched shirt. He carried himself with the quiet confidence of a true gentleman, nodding politely as he approached.

Relief rushed through Logan as the knot of tension loosened in his stomach. He went to meet Charles halfway and extended his hand. "You made it."

Charles gripped it firmly, smiling. "Wouldn't miss it for da world."

As they approached the table, Della stood and wrapped him in a quick hug. "It's wonderful to see you again, Charles. You look terrific."

Charles chuckled softly. "Not as terrific as you."

His family remained stoic, exchanging silent glances. No words. No nods. Just uniform blank expressions and an awkward silence.

Logan sat down with Della on his right and Charles on his left. He gently squeezed her hand, grateful to be sharing this evening with the two most important people in his life. No matter what happened tonight, he was determined to use his status as a finalist to his advantage, not just to promote his own work, but to uplift other talented artists on the island by featuring them in his gallery.

Throughout dinner, he split his attention between Della and Charles, savoring every shared laugh, every story, every glance that reminded him how far he'd come.

He exchanged smiles with Tarone, who sat with his arm around Lainey at the table with Pete LaMaur and his wife, Shakara, along with Shawn Wells and his wife, Lisa. In moments like this, surrounded by old friends, Logan couldn't help but feel grateful for their presence in his life.

After dessert and coffee were served, the room buzzed with anticipation as the awards ceremony began. Once the keynote speaker finished, the host moved on to the awards. One by one, categories were presented until finally, it was time for the last award of the night—the category of Painting.

Logan's heart pounded as the presenter listed the finalists. The moment stretched as the envelope was opened, the presenter paused, silently studying the results. Della squeezed his hand.

"And the winner is..." His face beamed. "Logan Chandler, for *Bittersweet Harvest*."

Gasps rippled through the crowd, followed by a hearty wave of applause. Logan's parents sat in stunned silence. Della let out a squeal and threw her arms around him. At the next table, Tarone and the others jumped to their feet, cheering and clapping.

Dazed, Logan rose and mechanically walked to the stage, stunned by the applause that thundered across the room. He accepted the award, shook hands with the presenter, and stepped up to the microphone.

"I'd like to thank the judges for believing in my work and honoring it with this award. I genuinely didn't expect to win, so this recognition is a profound and humbling surprise—one that I don't take lightly."

Logan paused to clear his throat, overcome with emotion. "I also want to express my deepest gratitude and appreciation to Charles Jefferson, my art instructor, my mentor, and a lifelong friend. His steady, guiding hand has always been there when I needed encouragement. Sometimes," he added with a grateful smile to the silent, enraptured crowd, "it came as a firm push in the right direction. He's a wise and patient teacher who saw something in me long before I saw it in myself. This award belongs to him just as much as it does to me. Thank you, Charles."

As Logan made his way back to the table amidst another flurry of applause and a standing ovation, people reached out to congratulate him with handshakes, hugs, and kind words. Tarone embraced him in a brotherly hug. Charles, overcome with emotion, extended a trembling hand.

But Logan didn't hesitate. He pulled Charles into a bear hug, tears burning in both their eyes.

After the closing remarks of the evening, Barb approached Logan, her expression a mix of admiration and surprise. "I never suspected that *Bittersweet Harvest* was yours. It's so different from your usual work. I just assumed you'd entered one of your coastal-themed watercolors," she said with a frown as if trying to reconcile the raw emotion of the painting with the artist she thought she knew.

Grant followed with a handshake and a half-smile. "Congratulations," he said. "Though I've gotta say... It's a bit controversial, don't you think?"

Logan simply nodded, unmoved. "Sometimes truth makes people uncomfortable," he replied boldly. "But that doesn't make it any less real."

Michelle ignored him, preoccupied with texting someone on her phone.

As the crowd began to thin, Logan turned to Della. "Hey," he said, leaning in slightly to be heard over the hum of conversation. "About the party at my parents' place... I know things didn't get off to the best start with them, but—are you still okay with going?"

"Of course," she replied sweetly. "I wouldn't want to be anywhere else."

He also reminded Charles, who smiled warmly at the kind gesture, but shook his head.

"Thank you, but I think I'll call it a night. I'm still an employee— and this is *your* night." Charles pushed his chair aside. "Gotta get moving. I'm driving da family home. I'll see you tomorrow."

Logan watched him go, his chest tight with gratitude. He turned back to Della, lacing his fingers with hers. "This turned out better with my parents than I thought it would," he remarked with a skeptical shrug, "but the night's not over."

No matter what anyone said—about the painting, the message, or his place in the world—he held his head high. The truth was out, and he stood by it. His work spoke for itself, and no one was going to dim his light.

Chapter Seventeen

The ride with Logan to the Chandler estate wound along the coastal highway. It had been a long day for Della, and the deep, rhythmic roar of the waves lapping along the shore eased her weariness. Resting her head against Logan's warm shoulder, she drifted toward sleep until his voice gently intruded on her blissful state.

"The museum wants to buy my painting," he said, sounding deep in thought. "The director, who is also the head curator, approached me after the ceremony ended and gave me his card. We only spoke briefly, but he wants to meet me for lunch next week at the museum to discuss the commission."

"Logan, that's wonderful," Della replied, sitting up straight.

"He says he has other daguerreotypes of that period that he'd like me to paint as well. He's putting together a collection of the LaBore family history for an exhibit, and he wants the paintings to help describe both the people and everyday life on the plantation." He held up his cast-covered wrist with a sigh. "I sure wish I hadn't done this. It's going to slow me down, and I'm really eager to start another oil painting."

"I'm so happy for you," Della replied, squeezing his arm. "I still remember how discouraged you were the day I met you on the ferry. I didn't understand why, but now I realize that the problem wasn't a lack of passion. You just needed to find the right story to tell. Something that spoke to the human heart."

"That's what Tarone said to me the night I ran into him at Nigel's," Logan mused. "On assignments all over the world, he captured images that he knew would shock people into caring about the lives they were seeing. It got me thinking, and I realized that's why I recreated that daguerreotype of the slaves working at the LaBore plantation. My paintings needed to evoke strong emotions in both me and the viewer to truly stand out. To make a difference." He sighed. "I've always known something was missing in my work. I just didn't realize until now what it was."

"Maybe that's why I've never found modern art very interesting," Della said honestly. "I just can't relate to a wall covered in giant paint splashes or a canvas with three colored stripes. It doesn't tell me anything."

The car veered sharply around a corner as if Logan had gotten so caught up in the conversation that he'd nearly missed a turn. Della looked up to find a winding gravel road overshadowed by a tropical canopy of tall, dark silhouettes that led up a steep hill. At the crest stood an imposing set of wrought iron gates, open wide and supported by stone pillars. They reminded her of the entrance to Graceland. In the distance, bathed in the glow of floodlights, a huge brick house stood majestically in the night.

Della stared at Barb and Grant Montclair's three-story house and its expansive, meticulous grounds in awe. *Who are these people, anyway?*

The car passed the circular drive in front of the house and took a side road, pulling into a large parking area across from a one-story house with huge windows framed with vines of brightly-colored bougainvillea. Soft lighting illuminated the sidewalks and pool area. The inside lights were on.

"Who lives in this smaller house," Della asked. "Is this your former residence?"

"That's the guest cottage," Logan replied, sounding distracted as he slid out of the car. He opened Della's car door and reached inside to assist her. "The party is at the main house."

Tiki torches lined the stone pathway to the main house, their flames flickering and dancing, leading guests toward the heart of the gathering. From the veranda, the shimmering tone of steel drums echoed the smooth pulse of reggae music through the grounds.

In the house, tall French doors in the living room stood wide open, welcoming the night air. Ceiling fans gently rotated overhead, the warm light spilling across polished stone floors, rosewood furniture, and accent tables inlaid with mother-of-pearl. Guests mingled about, their silhouettes moving easily among the rooms.

Della stared through the crowd of island dignitaries and museum board members in wonder, taking in the elegant swirl of sequined gowns and tuxedo-clad guests. Among them, servers in black and white attire circulated with trays of rum punch, mojitos, and sparkling wine, while an elegant buffet offered desserts, tropical fruits, and rich, freshly brewed coffee.

The scene felt a world away from anything she'd ever known.

Logan accepted two flutes of sparkling wine from a server and offered her a glass. He held up his flute with his free hand. "To success. Both of us."

"To success," Della chimed in and touched the rim of her crystal glass to his.

They wandered carefree through the crowd, greeting people and making polite conversation as people congratulated Logan on his win and his painting.

"There's someone I want you to meet," he murmured in her ear, guiding her toward a middle-aged man with a mustache wearing a tuxedo. His thinning, shoulder-length brown hair, pulled back into a ponytail, reminded Della of a successful artist from SoHo in lower Manhattan.

"Della, I'd like you to meet Harry Schneider, the owner of the Edgewater Gallery in Miami. He's returning to the island next week to discuss taking a few of my pieces on consignment and possibly a solo exhibition."

Hmmm… I wonder if you were one of the galleries who initially turned him down, Della thought as they shook hands. What an interesting turn of events.

Barb hurriedly approached them, her long black dress whispering with each step, diamonds glittering at her neck and wrists.

"Good evening, Mrs. Montclair," Della said sweetly. Barb simply ignored her.

"Logan, Sheriff Hall is at the door, and he wants to speak with you," Barb said in a low, irritated voice. "What did you do now?"

Logan blinked, his brows furrowing as though her rebuke had caught him off guard. "Nothing…that I know of."

Barb pursed her lips. "Well, take the conversation *outside*. I don't want him upsetting my guests."

"Of course," Logan said evenly and turned away from her.

"So much for making a good impression on her…" Della murmured to herself.

He and Della quickly excused themselves, promising to continue their conversation with Mr. Schneider as soon as they resolved their unexpected interruption and hastily made their way to the door.

"Sher-eeff Hall is waiting for you on the sidewalk," the tall doorman said with utmost politeness. He opened the door and ushered them outdoors.

Sheriff Hall stood away from the entrance, partially hidden by a tall hibiscus shrub as he smoked a cigarette. He flicked it into the dew-covered grass when they approached. "Duane, what's this about? Mom said you needed to speak with me."

"Actually, it's da little lady here that I need to speak with," the sheriff said. He looked gravely at Della. "Someone tried to burn down your store tonight."

Della gasped loudly. Her head swam with dizziness as she fought off the shock of his words. "Oh, my gosh! When? How? What do you mean, tried?"

"Don't worry," Sheriff Hall said gently and took her hands in his. "He didn't get a chance to start a blaze. I intercepted him before he could do any damage, but I'm afraid da back of your place has been doused with gasoline. I've got da fire department spraying it down with water as we speak."

Della gripped his hands tighter. "You caught him? Was it Vince Bernard?"

"I don't know." Sheriff Hall shook his head with frustration. "He saw me and ran. Got clean away."

"Even so," Logan remarked with surprise, "that was fantastic timing."

"Well, you see," the sheriff said, "ever since da perp tried to break in da back door of Miz Della's place, I've been watching downtown closely at night. I got a reserve officer watching Main Street, and I cover da alley. I was sitting in my cruiser in da hardware parking lot when I saw him run into her yard and start splashing gas on her back wall." He removed his hat and ran his hand over his closely cropped hair. "All dressed in black, of course, with a hoodie."

Logan extended his hand. "Thanks, Duane. I was worried it might come to something like this."

"Don't worry," Sheriff Hall said firmly, "we'll catch him."

Not if Lainey and I catch him first, Della thought as the sheriff tipped his hat and headed back to his cruiser. *Don't underestimate the power of a ticked-off woman. 'Da perp' is going to be dealing with two of us.*

They returned to the party, but Della didn't follow Logan to continue his conversation with Mr. Schneider. Instead, she wandered through the house in search of Lainey. She found her friend in the dining room with Tarone, munching on a pineapple tart.

"There's something I need to tell you," Della whispered as she glanced around. "But not here. Too many people."

Lainey pushed back her chair and stood. "What's up, girl?"

"Let's go outside."

Lainey grabbed her tart, finishing the last of it as she and Della went through the busy kitchen and out the back door. Following the stone path, they made their way to the wrought-iron pergola in the flower garden.

"Sheriff Hall was just here," Della exclaimed as they sat on cushioned benches, "and he said someone tried to burn down the salon by dousing the back wall with gasoline!"

Lainey gasped, clutching her hand to her chest, then she angrily let out a string of swear words. "Did he arrest the guy?"

"No." Della shook her head and let out a sigh of disappointment. "He got away. I sure wish we had the security cameras that Logan and Tarone have promised us!"

A black Mercedes rolled slowly along the side road. Della watched the car drive toward the guest house and stop, distinguishing its lights.

It's almost as if this person doesn't want to be noticed, she thought suspiciously.

A man opened the driver's side door and slid out, talking on a cell phone. She recognized him right away as the person who picked up Michelle the day she'd visited the salon.

"Who is that?" she asked Lainey as she pointed to the dark-haired man wearing black jeans and a dark T-shirt. "Do you recognize him?"

"Oh, that's Kirk Stroebel. He owns Hideaway Cove Resort. Vince Bernard works for him. What's he doing here at this hour?" Lainey mused, sounding curious.

Della stared hard at the man. "He's certainly not dressed for the party. My guess is that he doesn't want anyone to know he's here. I think he's meeting someone privately." She paused. "Logan's sister."

A look of disbelief flickered across Lainey's face. "Michelle?" she said, letting out a wry laugh. "No way. That snob wouldn't be caught dead with a lowlife like him. He drinks too much, and when he's sober, he struts around like some two-bit mob boss. He's got a history of abusing his girlfriends, too. Not many people on the island trust that guy."

Kirk Stroebel suddenly slipped his phone in his jeans pocket and headed for the pool adjacent to the guest house.

Moments later, Michelle Chandler appeared on the stone pathway, quietly slipping away in the same direction.

Lainey's eyes narrowed as she watched them converge and disappear. "My, oh my…what's she doing playin' around with a sleezy guy like *him*?"

Della stared at the guest house, wondering if something else was going on. "And during a party? With so many people here, the risk of getting interrupted is huge. I don't know, but something doesn't feel right here. If this guy is as bad as you say he is, I think we should snoop around. Make sure she's okay." She pulled out her phone. "I'm calling

Logan."

But he didn't answer his phone.

"I'll try Tarone," Lainey suggested, already dialing as they hurried to the guest house. They slipped into the gated pool area. The serene oval-shaped pool shimmered under soft lighting. The still surface of the water looked eerily calm. "He's probably with Logan."

The vertical fabric shade was pulled across the triple patio doors, but the door wasn't closed all the way. Raised voices filtered through the crack, sharp, heated—and so did the unmistakable stench of gasoline. Della slowly slid the door open a couple of inches and parted the panels of the shade with her fingers just enough to peer through. She froze.

The open-plan living space unfolded into a sunken living room anchored by a wall-sized TV, an overstuffed sofa, and a sleek, fully stocked bar. Off to the side, a modern kitchen merged seamlessly with the dining area. Michelle stood in her black, sparkly gown facing Kirk in front of the bar, tension etched across her face—a clear sign she was afraid of being discovered with him.

"They're on their way," Lainey whispered as she rejoined Della and craned her neck to watch the scene unfold.

"You shouldn't have come here," Michelle snapped in a shrill voice as she clenched her hands and paced the floor. "You smell like gasoline. It's too risky!"

"I just passed Duane on my way in, and he didn't circle back to pull me over and arrest me, so he doesn't suspect me," Kirk boasted arrogantly and opened the liquor cabinet, grabbing a fifth of premium-grade whiskey that was about a quarter full. "I had to get away fast. Some of it splashed on me when I dropped the can and ran off." He gave her a warning look. "No one knows about this but you and me, so keep your mouth shut."

She stopped short and spun around, her short blonde hair swinging across her face. "No one? Not even Vince Bernard?"

Kirk laughed harshly as he unscrewed the bottle and splashed a double shot into a lowball glass. "Are you kidding? The first time that idiot got drunk, he'd start bragging, and our plans would be all over town."

Della exchanged surprised looks with Lainey. "Vince had nothing to do with the vandalism? So, he *was* telling the truth when he denied it to me tonight," she whispered.

Lainey shrugged. "Guess so."

"I think we'd better cool it for a while," Michelle said in a worried tone. She folded her arms and leaned against the black marble countertop on the kitchen service island. "You escaped tonight, but Duane is gunning for us now, and he won't rest until he catches us."

Kirk tossed back the whiskey like it was water. "Not if we change the plan." He splashed more whiskey into his glass, filling it half-full this time and tossing it back without so much as a grimace. "Until now, we've been pulling pranks—amateur stuff. It's time we upped our game and did some serious damage to Main Street's reputation." He deftly slipped one spaghetti strap off her shoulder, caressing her soft, creamy skin with his fingers.

Della cast a sideways glance at Lainey. Her business partner's expression had turned to stone.

Michelle jerked the strap back into place and pushed him away. "I don't want you too drunk to drive home," she retorted as she snatched the glass from Kirk's hand and set it firmly on the counter. "If you get pulled over and the cop smells gas, it's all over. Now, what are you talking about?"

Pinning her back against the counter with his hands braced on both sides, Kirk loomed over her, his frown twisting into an ugly scowl. "Don't *ever* tell me what to do." He grabbed the uncapped bottle, as if daring her to stop him again. "I'm going to tap a few guys from Miami to rob the merchants at gunpoint and stage muggings on the street in broad daylight. We'll target your precious brother first. After that, it won't take much convincing to get your parents to side with me against the grant program. We'll demand it be pulled until the suspects are caught—which will never happen."

Michelle shook her head vehemently. "I was happy to help you spray paint storefronts and write a threatening note, but this? It's criminal! What's the matter with you, Kirk? When I said I'd help you force the merchants downtown to go out of business, I never agreed to take things that far!"

Kirk lifted the bottle to his lips, drained it, and set it back on the counter. "Look, you *do* want Logan to give up and come back to the firm, don't you?"

"Yes, but not that way. I just want to get rid of that brainless twit from Minnesota," Michelle said in a huff. "As long as she's on the island, my brother won't leave. She keeps encouraging him to turn his back on us and waste his life painting those dime-store pictures. She *has* to go!"

Della had heard enough. She pulled the patio door open all the way, parted the panels of the vertical blind, and marched into the room. "I heard everything you said. How dare you try to destroy my business! How dare you try to frighten me away! Well, I'm not leaving. Instead, I plan to make sure everyone knows what you've done." Her gaze locked on Michelle's. "*Especially* you, turning against your own brother. When Logan finds out how badly you've betrayed him, he won't just walk away from you. He'll never look back."

At first, Kirk and Michelle stared at her, too stunned to respond. Then Kirk laughed. "It's your word against ours. Two business owners who donate a lot of money to island preservation, or a newcomer looking for a handout. Who do you think people will believe?"

She stared back at him defiantly. "*Me.*"

He moved close, staring down at her with a menacing glare as he grabbed her arm and shoved her against the wall, gripping his large hand around her neck. "Don't get sassy with me, you stupid Chandler whore. I could snap your neck right now with one hand. Dump you in the sea. No one would ever find your body."

Michelle grabbed his free arm and tried to pull him away. "Kirk! No!" she screamed. "This is crazy!"

With a violent swing of his arm, he thrust Michelle away. "I warned you not to tell me what to do."

She fell to the floor and began to sob.

"Hey! Leave her alone!" Della shouted and thrust her knee between his legs.

He grunted and doubled over, gasping for breath. "Why, you little—"

He never knew what hit him. From behind, Lainey raised her arm and smashed the empty whiskey bottle over his head. The bottle broke into shards, scattering everywhere as his knees buckled, and he collapsed to the floor.

Lainey stood over him, her eyes blazing. "Chandler whore? That'll teach you to disrespect my friend."

Della ran to the kitchen area and retrieved two frying pans hanging on hooks above the countertop range. She handed one to Lainey as they both stood guard over him. "Kirk Stroebel," she announced forcefully. "You are under Citizen's Arrest!"

Chapter Eighteen

Logan spotted Harry Schneider deep in conversation with one of the museum board members and decided not to interrupt him. If they didn't get a chance tonight to finish their discussion, they could catch up next week when Harry visited his gallery.

Grant stood in the doorway to his office and motioned for Logan to speak with him. His grave expression made it clear they were about to *have words* over something.

Now what, Logan thought with irritation. *Did my acceptance speech offend you because I publicly lauded Charles as the true father figure in my life and not you?*

Once inside Grant's study, a small, square room filled with custom-made bookshelves and an ornate rosewood desk, Logan stood before him, wondering what Grant was going to lecture him for this time. "What's this all about? What did I do now?"

Grant unhooked his bow tie and tugged it loose. "I understand you had a conversation with Tom Boyce about purchasing your painting."

The inquiry, spoken like an accusation, tripped Logan's temper like a switch. "Yeah, I did. He also wants me to paint a few more for him from daguerreotypes in the museum archives. We're meeting next Wednesday to finalize the details." Logan met Grant's gaze, steady and unflinching. "Why? You got a problem with that, too?"

"The museum director doesn't have the authority to make financial decisions over five hundred dollars without authorization from the Board." Grant rolled up the bowtie and stuffed it in his pocket. "He's overstepped his bounds."

Logan shrugged. "I disagree. He said the Board meets on Monday night, and it would be no problem getting the request approved."

"He takes a lot for granted," Grant growled as he loosened the top button of his starched white shirt. "Not everyone is in favor of purchasing that painting."

Heat began to climb the back of Logan's neck. He had all he could do to keep his voice level. "And just who else have you persuaded to vote no concerning my commission?"

"Look, Logan," Grant argued, moving behind his desk. "Don't take this personally. It's not about your skill as an artist—"

"Then what is it?" Logan shot back. "Do you find the painting offensive? Embarrassing? Or simply too amateur for your taste?"

Grant's face flushed at the accusations as he placed his palms on the desk and leaned forward. "As I said, it's not about you or your talent, Logan. It's about the integrity of the museum. That picture is a stain on the island's history."

"That picture *is* the island's history." Logan snapped. "And it needs to be acknowledged. Knowing how outspoken Anna LaBore was back when she was alive, I have no doubt she would have agreed!"

Grant eased into his office chair and folded his hands on the desk, as if trying to regain control of the conversation. "I'm not going to argue with you," he said authoritatively. "I just wanted to give you a heads-up that Monday night's board meeting might not go the way you'd like."

Realizing he was being dismissed, Logan headed for the door. He paused, then turned back. "Yeah, well, we'll see about that." He angled his head slightly. "Nothing personal."

I won't just make them believe in my painting, he thought, his resolve hardening. *I'll make them believe in me. My future depends on it.*

Logan left Grant's study, searching for Della. He needed to vent, and she was the first person he wanted to talk to. He always felt better after confiding in her. Room by room, he wandered through the house but couldn't find either Della or Lainey. Where were they?

Tarone suddenly appeared. "Logan, we gotta go to the guest house," he blurted, sounding worried. "Lainey and Della need us— now!"

"What's going on?" Logan shouted as they tore through the kitchen and ran out the back door.

"I don't know, but Lainey sounded majorly upset!"

They sprinted across the backyard and burst through the gate, then charged into the house.

Inside, Lainey and Della stood over Kirk Stroebel, gripping heavy frying pans as makeshift weapons. Della's face looked pale. Red blotches in the form of a handprint covered her neck.

Kirk slumped on the floor, dazed, clutching his bloodied head. The pungent stench of gasoline clung to him.

"Della!" Logan said as he hurried toward her. "Are you okay?"

She swallowed hard. "Yeah…"

"Get these witches away from me!" Kirk bellowed, shielding the crown of his bloody head with his hand. "They attacked me. I'm bleeding!"

Tarone rushed to Lainey's side and gently removed the pan from her hands. He slid his arm around her and pulled her close. "You're safe now, babe. You don't need this."

"Darn, you're no fun," Lainey complained as she surrendered the pan. "I was waiting for jerk-face to make a wrong move..."

Logan took the pan from Della's trembling hands and set it on the counter. Wrapping his arms around her protectively, he held her close. "I don't understand what's going on here. Why did you hit him?"

"Lainey did—because he threatened me," she whispered unsteadily.

"...what?" Logan's voice, rough with fury, sounded as deadly serious as he felt. Seething with murderous anger, he locked gazes with Kirk. "If you *ever* threaten her again..." he said, each word as sharp as steel, "I swear, I'll make you regret it."

Michelle let out a loud moan. She sat curled in a ball on the sofa, holding her face in her hands, and began sobbing uncontrollably.

"Michelle?" Noticing her for the first time, Logan hurried to his sister's side and knelt in front of her, gently gripping her shoulders. "Hey, what's wrong?" Logan's head snapped up. "Stroebel, if you hurt my sister—"

"He shoved her to the floor, but that's not why she's crying," Della said sharply. "She's going to jail."

Logan froze. "Wait...what?" He shook his head in disbelief. "What are you talking about?"

"She helped vandalize our salon. And your gallery." Della jabbed a finger in Kirk's direction. "He tried to burn down my salon tonight." She scrunched her nose. "The stench of gasoline gives him away."

Logan blinked, unable to fathom what he was hearing. "That can't be. Michelle would *never* do something like that. Not to me." He turned to his sister. "Would you, Michelle?"

"We witnessed their argument about it," Lainey chimed in. "She was happy to go along with the plan until Kirk wanted to hire thugs to rob us in broad daylight and mug innocent shoppers to make downtown appear unsafe."

Why would Michelle... Logan's thoughts churned, confusion tightening in his chest as his heart began to sink. *No, not Michelle!*

"I don't put anything past him," he said, staring hard at Kirk, "but my sister..." He glanced at Michelle and shook his head. "She wouldn't do that to me."

Della winced as though it grieved her to reveal the truth. "She did," she said softly, her voice edged with the sadness and anger that only resulted from betrayal. "Sheriff Hall is on his way."

Reeling with disbelief, Logan sat next to his sister. "Is that true, Michelle? Look at me."

She lifted her head; her eyes were red and puffy from crying. "I never meant for anyone to get hurt, Logan. I just wanted you to stop fiddling with that gallery and come back to work at the firm. Ever since you quit, Mom and Grant have shifted more accounts to Jon and me. We argue with them constantly about it, and now Jon's threatening to leave, too. That's why he was a no-show tonight. He's angry with Mom and Grant. Our family is breaking apart!"

The constant pressure to do more and more is why I left, Logan thought bitterly to himself. *I never had enough time or energy left over to do the things I loved. That's why I won't go back.*

Stunned, he moved away from her, his heart aching with the weight of her betrayal.

Flashing red and blue lights reflected against the wall, announcing the arrival of a police vehicle. Logan glanced out the living room window just as an ambulance pulled up behind the cruiser.

Sheriff Hall quickly entered through the patio doors. Two male EMTs followed on his heels. He surveyed the area intently, taking in details of the scene as he sternly approached the group. "So, what do we have here?"

"*Here* is your downtown vandal," Della said, stepping forward. "He's the one you almost caught tonight in the act of trying to torch my building."

The sheriff sniffed the air. "He sure smells like it. We'll check his shoes to confirm a match from da prints we took from da scene." He glanced at Kirk's footwear. "Retro Air Jordan sneakers, possibly size eleven, with a distinctive tread. Hmmm… Don't know many people on this island who can afford a luxury like that." He tilted his head. "They look like a match to me. Kirk Stroebel, I'm arresting you on suspicion of arson—"

"And assault!" Lainey added, pointing to the red marks on Della's neck where Kirk's hand had held her against her will.

"I didn't do it! They're lying," Kirk bellowed. "This is harassment and false arrest. You'll be hearing from my lawyer!"

"That's between you, da judge, and da evidence," Sheriff Hall replied calmly, stepping aside as the EMTs moved in to assist Kirk into a wheelchair. "Let's get you into da ambulance and get that cut on your head checked out first. I suspect there will be additional charges by the time you're released into my custody."

As the EMTs eased him into the wheelchair, the sheriff began reading Kirk his Miranda Rights.

Guests from the party crowded the doorway, whispering among themselves.

Sheriff Hall turned to Michelle. "As for you, my dear, I'd like you to come with me to the station tonight."

Barb Montclair burst through the crowd. "Logan, what's going on here? What happened to Kirk?" She rushed to Michelle. "My darling, are you all right?"

"Mom—" Logan began, but she turned away to question the sheriff.

Sheriff Hall explained the circumstances.

Barb listened with stony disapproval. "This is an outrage. You have no right to arrest her for anything." She turned to Logan. "Fetch Grant. *Now.* We'll settle this thing immediately."

Still angry with his stepfather, Logan did as his mother requested and pulled out his phone, dialing Grant's number. When Grant answered, Logan said briskly, "You're needed at the guest house. There's been an incident. Get out here. *Now.*"

He hung up and shoved the phone back into his pocket as Barb launched into a tirade against Sheriff Hall. Leaving no insult or threat unsaid, she ordered him and his associates to vacate the premises.

Ignoring her outburst, Logan slid his arm around Della and drew her close. The red marks on her neck would soon become dark bruises. She was his only concern, not Kirk, not Michelle, or his issues with Grant. "How are you feeling?" he murmured, brushing a stray hair from her face. "I'll take you to the station to give your statement."

She didn't answer.

Concern tugged at his heart, and he pulled her into a gentle hug. She was just overwhelmed, he reasoned, and exhausted.

"You," Barb said, motioning to Della and Lainey. "This is all your doing, and I'd like you to leave. You've caused enough trouble for one evening."

"Mom!" Logan exclaimed, embarrassed by her tactless behavior. "It's not their fault!"

"Yes, ma'am," Lainey said mockingly and grabbed Tarone by the hand. "Y'all sure know how to give an entertaining party."

"You're following me to da station," Sheriff Hall instructed the girls. "I need to get your statements."

Outside, the large crowd that had gathered began to disperse, murmuring among themselves that it was their time to leave as well.

"Let's go," Logan said, his earlier triumph at the awards ceremony now a distant memory.

He and Della stepped outside just as Grant arrived, his face twisted with anger. "Who called the cops? Can't you stay out of trouble for *one* evening? Where's your mother?"

"She's inside," Logan muttered, walking Della past him without slowing. "Probably calling around for a good criminal attorney."

They got as far as the side road when Della stopped. "I don't want you to drive me to the station," she said, surprising him. "I'll go with Lainey and Tarone."

"No," he replied stubbornly, ignoring the slamming of car doors, the flashing of lights, and engines revving in the parking area. "I'll take you. I want to be there for you."

She pulled her hand away and folded her arms, a gesture as final as closing a door. "I'd rather go with Lainey. I—I don't think we're right for each other."

The resolve in her voice shocked him. He blinked, disoriented as if the ground had shifted beneath his feet. "Della, you don't mean that. This has been a long and trying day, and you've been through a frightening ordeal. You're just tired."

"If anything," she argued, "what happened tonight opened my eyes to the truth." She glanced at the parking area, scanning for Tarone's car as though she couldn't get away fast enough. "Look, what I mean is, it's bad enough that your parents don't think I'm good enough for you, and your sister tried to destroy my business, but when I told you the truth about her tonight, you didn't believe me. You argued for her innocence." Her voice trembled. "Yeah, I get that you don't want to believe bad things about Michelle, but you're loyal to her because she's family. And you always will be because it's the right thing to do. But where does that leave me? Always struggling to prove myself to people who don't like me? Always trying to be good enough for you? I can't live like that."

"That's not true, Della!" Logan exclaimed from his heart. "Maybe I'm not good enough for *you*. I don't care what they think. I don't care about my award or the board or the gallery or any of it—including the firm. All I care about is you because…I've fallen in love with you."

She backed away like his words hurt more than they healed. "Maybe I've fallen in love with you, too," she said, tears streaking her face, "but that doesn't change the fact that there's more wrong with us than what is right."

When he reached for her, she flinched, then gently pushed his hand away. "You've got more important things to deal with right now than me. Your sister is in serious trouble, and she needs you. Go straighten things out with your family and… just forget me."

She turned and ran toward Tarone's car, waving at him to stop.

"Della!" Logan called after her. "Della, wait!"

She didn't look back.

As her silhouette disappeared into the blur of taillights and rising dust, Logan stood frozen in the shadows—alone, his heart shattered, and unsure how to put the pieces back together.

Chapter Nineteen

Della sprinted to Tarone's car and jerked open the back door as it slid to a stop. She dove into the back seat and slammed the door, staring at the floor to prevent Tarone and Lainey from seeing her tears.

"Logan not coming?" Tarone asked gently, glancing into the rear-view mirror. He frowned. "Are you okay?"

Della nodded but didn't speak. A small sob escaped her lips.

"Logan must be staying back with his family," Lainey murmured to Tarone. "I wish we didn't have to give our statements to the police tonight, but it's important, so it's better to get it over with."

She turned to Della. "We need to stay until they get photos of the bruises on your neck. Okay?"

"Yeah," Della whispered, her voice thick with fatigue. She wanted Kirk to be prosecuted for what he'd done to her, but tonight, she was too emotionally drained to think about justice. All she wanted was to go home, soak in her claw-foot tub, and let the hot water ease her frayed nerves. Soothe her broken heart.

Her phone buzzed. It was Logan. Wincing at the sight of his name, she declined the call and slipped it back into her black satin evening bag. Unless something drastically changed, she had nothing to say to him. Not tonight. Maybe not ever.

Lainey reached into the back seat and gently patted her shoulder. The knowing look in her eyes made it clear she knew Della had ended things with Logan. "You've had a rough day, hon," She murmured with a soft, sympathetic sigh. "I'm so sorry."

You have no idea, Della thought, her heart aching. She truly believed what they had was real. Logan had confessed that he loved her, but when it mattered the most, he failed to show it. Tears flowed down her cheeks again, filled with grief and heartbreaking disappointment. *It's going to take me a long time to get over him.*

Tarone and Lainey were silent all the way to the station, giving her space to calm down. At the station, she mumbled through her statement and sat like a zombie while an officer took photos of the bruises on her neck. On her way out, she spotted Barb and Grant in the lobby, waiting for their lawyer. Grant scowled and paced the floor. Barb looked the other way.

Della ignored them and kept her gaze focused straight ahead as she quickly passed by, treating them like strangers—because by their own choice, they were.

As the station's glass doors whooshed shut behind her, Della stepped into the balmy night and lifted her gaze to the stars scattered across the sky. The ache of breaking up with Logan lingered, sharp and undeniable. But it also brought clarity.

She'd lost him. But she still had herself.

And her dream still mattered—now more than ever.

She hadn't come to the island for love. She came to build a future, and it was time to pour everything she had into the salon—the one thing that truly belonged to her.

No more distractions. No more doubt. From now on, she was all in.

Late April – Easter Weekend

Della and Lainey closed the salon at noon on Good Friday.

"Are you excited about your family being here for the weekend?" Lainey asked Della as she swept hair clippings on the floor. Lainey's family always went to church together in the late afternoon and came back home afterward for a traditional family dinner. This year, she had invited Tarone to join her.

Zeus lay curled up on his blanket in the corner, snoring and passing gas.

"Yeah," Della chirped and gathered up her scissors to have them sharpened at the hardware store across the alley. "Mom and Dad are very impressed with the Morganville Hotel. Shawn and Lisa have gone out of their way to make them feel welcome." She laughed. "Even Christina is happy with their service, and that says something!"

Being the cost-conscious couple that they were, Rachel and Bill Delaney had first tried to get rooms at Elsie's B&B, but the entire house had been rented to a single family for the weekend months ago.

Lainey paused, leaning against the broom. "Speaking of Christina, where is your sister? I thought by now that girl would be here bugging you to go shopping or to go to the beach with her."

Della shut off the coffeemaker, then picked up the glass coffee pot and dumped out its contents in the shampoo bowl. "She slept in and had room service for breakfast. After I styled her hair, she said she was going to spend some time in the hotel gift shop." She turned on the cold water and rinsed the pot. "I'm surprised my parents haven't dropped by yet. They get up at the crack of dawn, so they must be pretty bored by now."

"Maybe not," Lainey said seriously. "Your mom asked me last night, after we were introduced, if there were any furniture stores on the island. I told her the only places to buy furnishings were either the thrift store or the hardware store. I think they went shopping."

Della placed the pot back on the coffeemaker. "She couldn't wait to see my apartment last night when I met them at the pier." She paused. "Mom was shocked by how little furniture I had. I'm sure glad my new loveseat arrived on time, so she at least had somewhere to sit!" She laughed. "I think she's home shopping for me."

The door chime jingled with the tinkle of a dinner bell as it slid open, and Christina breezed in wearing a short, white sundress accented with a huge Tanzanite filigree pendant and matching earrings. Della recognized the expensive set as one of Shakara's exclusive creations. The shampoo and blow-dry that Della had given her sister's long, coppery tresses earlier still glistened like silk.

Zeus rose and trotted toward her, his tail wagging.

She ignored the dog. "Hey, there, sis. Good morning, Lainey! Like my new dress?" Christina twirled around for their approval. "I bought it at the hotel gift shop." She fondled the pendant. "This, too. Isn't it absolutely to die for?"

"Shakara is a very talented artist," Lainey replied. "And an amazing person, too."

"Speaking of artists," Christina said with a sigh, "I met the most dreamy guy at the art gallery on the next block. *Logan Chandler.*" She spoke his name in awe, like she'd just met a movie star. "I bought a painting from him and had it delivered to the hotel. He didn't even have to sweet-talk me into it. I've never been into the California surfer type, but he had me at 'Hello' with all that curly blonde hair and those stunning hazel eyes. That gorgeous smile…"

Della leaned against the countertop and glanced at Lainey. She hadn't spoken to Logan since that night at his parents' estate, and she didn't want to talk about him now. The pain of their breakup still ached deep in her heart. Since then, she'd managed to keep her mind off him by concentrating on building her business. Her efforts had paid off handsomely with the local gals by offering specials and by making appointments whenever a customer called, regardless of the day or time.

Business was becoming brisk for her and Lainey with repeat customers who got their hair and nails done the same day. Island Glow Hair Salon was building a reputation for great service, excellent coffee, and the go-to place for the newest gossip.

Christina caught the exchange of looks between Della and Lainey. "What's the matter? Do you know him?" She frowned. "What is it? Is he a real jerk or something?"

Lainey cleared her throat and got busy sweeping.

"We used to be…friends," Della said hesitantly. "Good friends. But it didn't work out."

"What? My little sister was having a fling with the island heartthrob?" Christina probed, becoming more intently interested.

Della let out an embarrassed laugh. "It-it wasn't like that."

"I'll bet it was." Christina smiled, her eyes sparkling over the discovery of her younger sister's secret. "What happened? Why aren't you together now?"

Della shrugged, indifferent. "Our priorities went in different directions."

Christina cut her sister a wry, no-nonsense look. "Nix the excuses, Della. What really happened?"

Della wandered over to the product shelf and began to rearrange the bottles. "If you really must know, Logan's family thought I was a bad influence on him."

"You?" Christina countered with a snort. "A bad influence? You're the epitome of Rebecca of Sunnybrook Farm. What'd you do, talk him out of going into the priesthood or something?"

Lainey let out a belly laugh.

Della glared at Lainey and turned back to her sister. "No, I sort of encouraged him to pursue his love of art instead of going back to his job working at his family's firm."

The front door opened with a loud jingle, and Rachel and Bill Delaney burst into the shop, laughing about something. Bill wore khaki cargo shorts, and a yellow shirt printed with palm fronds. Rachel had on light blue jean shorts and a matching light blue knit top.

Della and Christina clammed up instantly—a practice they'd perfected as kids whenever their parents interrupted a confidential conversation. Especially if it involved boys, which had *always* been considered top secret.

"I'm going back to the hotel to get ready for dinner tonight," Christina said, brushing past them toward the door. "See you later!"

Bill held up several large bags, grinning proudly. "We've been shopping!"

"We went to that nice thrift store a couple of blocks away," Rachel added, her voice brimming with excitement, "and I found the prettiest hand-crocheted doilies for your apartment. And look at this. Isn't it cute?" She held up a hollow ceramic frog with a wide opening in its back. "A place to store your dish scrubber!"

Well, it could be worse, Della thought. *At least it wasn't that copper raccoon with a clock in its belly.*

A loud vehicle rumbled up to the back door.

Bill set down his bags and hustled toward the noise, Zeus trotting behind him. "That's the delivery man!"

The delivery man turned out to be Joseph from the hardware store, driving a four-wheeler with a small trailer hitched to the back. The tall, lanky man with caramel-colored skin jumped out of his vehicle and pulled off his trucker hat, revealing expertly woven cornrows, Lainey's handiwork. "Hello, Miz Della. I brought your surprise."

Oh-oh, she thought worriedly, but her concern quickly faded.

Joseph pulled the tarp off his trailer and revealed several boxes containing a pair of rattan end tables and two small Tiffany-style accent lamps. He grinned proudly. "I saw you looking at these last week," he said proudly. "They were sold out then, but more just came in. Told your mamma right away."

Della smiled with a mix of relief and delight. "Thanks, Mom! Thanks, Dad!"

Bill and Joseph began carrying the boxes upstairs to her postage-stamp of a living room. It would be a tight fit, but they would look perfect on either side of her new loveseat.

Lainey glanced at her watch. "My goodness, it's twelve-thirty already. I'd better get going. Mamma will tan my backside if I don't get home in time to help her get ready for company," she said as she took off her apron and turned to Rachel. "Mrs. Delaney, I spoke to Mamma about the schedule for this afternoon. She said to come by around two-thirty for fresh-baked hot cross buns and coffee. At three-thirty, we'll walk over to church—Mamma likes to get there early on holidays to get a good seat. Dinner will be at five-thirty. We're having deep-fried grouper tonight. It's our family's Good Friday tradition."

She grabbed her purse from a lower cabinet and paused. "Tarone will pick you all up at the hotel."

Rachel thanked her and said the family would wait for Tarone in the lobby at two-fifteen. She thanked Lainey again and went upstairs to inform her husband.

"See you at two-thirty!" Lainey said to Della as she grabbed her purse and hurried out the back with Zeus in tow.

After Lainey and Joseph left, Rachel and Bill said goodbye and returned to the hotel to get ready for dinner. Bill promised to be back early on Saturday to unbox everything and assemble the tables.

Della opened the door to see them out so she could shower and get dressed in time, but she froze as Barb Montclair approached the salon dressed for church in a fitted black dress cinched with a silver belt and a black, wide-brimmed hat to match. Diamonds glittered at her neck and ears, catching the sunlight with every step. Her stride was purposeful, but her eyes were clouded with worry. What on earth did she want now? A little Good Friday retribution?

"Della," Barb asked stiffly, "may we talk?"

Della hesitated. Talk? About what? She hadn't seen Logan's mother since the night she passed both Barb and Grant Montclair at the police station and received a cold, silent dismissal. Did this have anything to do with Michelle?

"Okay," she said, puzzled, holding the door open. "May I ask what this is about?"

Barb's designer spiked heels clicked loudly on the tile floor as she entered the salon. She spun around. "I—I'd like to apologize to you for the way I treated you the night of the awards ceremony and at the party afterward," she blurted, her expression tense. "I was rude and insensitive. It was uncalled for." Her hands trembled slightly. Her voice held a note of desperation. "You're a sweet girl, Della. I had no right to treat you so callously, and I beg your forgiveness."

Barb's confession stunned her. *Oh, my gosh,* she thought in amazement. *What brought this on?* Something was wrong. Something more than this woman was revealing.

"I've never held it against you," Della replied softly. "After that night, I let it go, and since then, I've never looked back. I came to the island to start a business. Not make enemies."

Barb's eyes welled with tears. "I wish I could say the same. That night, I made an enemy of my son. He won't speak to me until I—"

"Logan?" Della cut in, surprised. "That doesn't sound like him at all. What do you mean?"

Barb clutched her Prada handbag and flinched slightly at the question. "We used to be so close as a family, but now my children are pulling away from Grant and me, and it breaks my heart. Both of my sons have left the firm, and my daughter…" Reaching into her purse, she pulled out a tissue and dabbed at her nose. "Logan blames Grant and me for what happened between the two of you. He refuses to have anything to do with us unless we make it right with you."

The high and mighty Barbara Montclair reduced to begging for forgiveness? Well, at least she picked the right day. But did she really mean it, or was this just a temporary ploy to make amends with her son? Della clasped her hands together to keep from revealing just how uncomfortable she found this encounter. "I accept your apology, Mrs. Montclair, with no hard feelings whatsoever, but I don't understand why it matters anymore. Logan and I…we're over."

"Not as far as he's concerned," Barb said gravely. "He's still in love with you."

Della stared at her, stunned. Something in her heart stirred. "How do you know this?"

"He's supposed to be creating several paintings for the LaBore Museum, but he's not working on them. I don't know if he's even touched the canvases yet." Barb shook her head. Her voice was threaded with frustration. "He spends all day working on a portrait of you."

Della blinked in surprise. "I didn't know that. Tarone and Lainey have never said a word to me about it."

They probably wanted to spare my feelings…

"Go to him, Della," Barb pleaded, stepping closer and taking Della's hands in hers. "If you don't love him anymore, then tell him so.

You'll break his heart, but at least then he can start to heal." Her eyes filled with tears. "I want my son back."

She walked to the door and slipped out without saying another word, leaving Della standing in shocked silence.

Della's thoughts churned as Barb walked out the door without looking back, leaving a storm of questions in her wake.

She stared at the door for a long moment, then slowly turned and sank onto the nearest chair. Her hands lay still in her lap while her thoughts spun like a carousel.

He's still in love with me?

She hadn't dared to hope—not after everything that had happened. Not after all this time.

But now…

She shot to her feet and walked straight out of the salon, not bothering with her purse, not even locking the door behind her.

I just want to tell him that Barb apologized to me, she told herself as she headed toward Main Street Gallery. *That's all. Maybe ask about the portrait.*

It was a simple excuse, a way to break the ice. To see his face. To find out if what Barb said was true.

And to confirm that he had chosen her over everything else.

Della's feet hit the pavement with purpose, her sandals slapping against the warm sidewalk as she headed toward Main Street Gallery. At first, her stride was steady, measured, but with every step, her thoughts raced faster. Her pulse quickened. Her pace matched her urgency.

She didn't know what she'd say to him when she saw him. She just knew she had to see him one more time.

By the time Main Street Gallery came into view, she was practically running.

She paused briefly at the door, hesitating long enough to catch her breath, then pushed it open. A chime echoed above her as she stepped inside, the cool air brushing against her flushed skin.

Logan stood in front of an easel near the window, brush in hand, completely absorbed in whatever he was painting. His hair was a little more tousled than usual, his shirt streaked with color. The sunlight filtering through the glass bathed him in soft gold.

He looked up at the sound of the door. Their gazes met. And for a moment, the world stopped moving.

Heat rushed through her chest like a wave—too many emotions, too fast to name. He didn't smile. He didn't speak. He just stared at her, like he wasn't sure she was real.

Her breath caught in her throat. *Barb wasn't lying.*

The truth of it was in his eyes—clear, raw, and heartbreakingly open.

He still loved her.

Della took slow steps forward, the soft tapping of her sandals echoing in the quiet room. "I didn't know if you'd be here," she said, her voice barely above a whisper. "But... I'm glad I checked."

Logan didn't move, didn't speak. His brush stayed frozen midair, his gaze locked on her like he was afraid she'd vanish if he blinked.

She swallowed hard, trying to find the right place to begin.

"Your mother came to see me," she said gently. "Just now. She... apologized."

Logan blinked, lowering the brush slightly.

"She said she was wrong about me. About everything." Della let out a shaky breath. "She told me you haven't been speaking to her since the night Michelle was arrested, and she blamed me for it. She said you asked her to make things right."

He set the brush down with quiet care and stepped out from behind the easel, the painting forgotten.

"I didn't ask," he said, his voice low. "I told her the only way I'd have anything to do with them again was if they treated you with the respect you deserve."

Della's eyes burned, but she didn't look away. "She also said...you've been painting a portrait of me."

Logan nodded slowly. "Every day. It's the only thing I can do that makes any sense right now."

She took another step toward him, her heart pounding.

"I came here to tell you she apologized," she said, her voice soft but steady. "But I think... I also came because I needed to see if what she said was true. That you were still in love with me."

His eyes searched hers. "And is it?"

"I don't know yet," she whispered, tears threatening. "But I want to find out."

Logan crossed the room in two long strides and stopped in front of her. Close enough to feel the heat between them still smoldering beneath everything left unsaid.

"I've loved you ever since the night you ran away from your apartment, frightened, to get away from the intruder. And you came to me. You trusted me," he said, his voice breaking with the weight of it. "My heart nearly stopped when you called me and said someone was trying to break in. I knew then that if anything ever happened to you, a part of me would die too."

Della let out the breath she hadn't realized she'd been holding. Her heart ached, but in a different way now—so full it almost hurt. She reached up and gently brushed her fingers against his paint-smeared sleeve. "Then let's figure this out. Together."

He pulled her into his arms and kissed her, tenderly at first, like he was afraid this might be the only chance he'd ever get to hold her again. But as the seconds stretched, the kiss deepened—slowly, then all at once—growing more desperate, more aching, as if he were trying to pour all his sorrow and longing into that one moment. When he finally pulled back, his eyes shimmered with emotion. "The only way I could survive being without you was to paint you. It was the only way I could still feel close to you. The only way I could breathe."

Della exhaled shakily, her heart aching in a way that felt both fragile and full. "Why didn't you tell me all of this?" she whispered. "I was only a block and a half away."

"When you stopped taking my calls, I thought I'd lost you for good. And maybe I deserved it, but I couldn't stop loving you. Not for a second." His arms tightened around her, and this time, she let herself fall into the warmth of it—into the truth of what they still had.

"There's something I want to show you," he said softly.

He took her by the hand and led her across the gallery to the easel by the window.

Della drew in a sharp breath.

It really was her.

The painting was based on a photo Tarone had taken of her the night of the awards ceremony. She looked regal in her elegant strapless gown, her long hair draped about her shoulders, her eyes sparkling with anticipation, framed by soft lighting that gave her an almost ethereal glow. In the painting, she wasn't just beautiful, she was luminous, alive with strength, courage, and something deeper. Something fragile, too.

She stepped closer, her chest tightening. "Oh, Logan…"

"I saw that picture on Tarone's phone after the ceremony," he said quietly. "And I couldn't stop thinking about how beautiful you looked. How brave. I've been working on this painting of you ever since that day."

"No one's ever… seen me like this before."

"I just paint what I see."

She reached for his hand and held it tightly in hers.

"My parents are here for the weekend. You've met my sister already," she said happily, then made a face. "I'd like you to meet Mom and Dad, too. We're going to Lainey's house tonight to attend church together and afterward for dinner," she said. "I'd like you to be there. With me."

He blinked, surprised. "You sure?"

She nodded. "If we're going to figure this out, we don't do it in pieces. We start now. You and me."

A slow, full smile spread across his face—one she hadn't seen in a long time. "I can't think of anyone else I'd rather be with tonight."

She smiled happily, her fingers lacing with his. "Good. Just don't get too friendly with Christina if you want to stay on my good side. She thinks you're dreamy and would love to steal you away from me."

"Thanks for the warning!" he said with a lighthearted laugh, and for the first time in weeks, the air between them felt easy again. "I'm going to be too busy stuffing myself with Mamma Clarke's deep-fried grouper to notice her flirting. Mamma C makes the best fish dinner on the island." He pulled her close and kissed her deeply, then pressed his lips to her ear. "Your sister is pretty and charming," he murmured, "but she's not you. *You're* the one I love."

Della's heart swelled as she smiled at him. "I love you too," she whispered, the words slipping out as naturally as breathing—true, certain, and long overdue.

They locked up the gallery and walked out hand in hand. Whatever came next, they'd face it together. And this time, they were all in.

The End

A note from Denise

Thank you so much for reading ***Della,*** *Book One of the Enchanted Island Series.* If you enjoyed this story, please take a moment to post a rating or short review on Amazon. Thank you! I appreciate it very much! Ratings and/or reviews help me to reach more people who love to read sweet romance.

To be notified when a new book is available, be sure to follow me on Amazon!

About the Author

Denise Devine is a USA Today bestselling author who has had a passion for books since the second grade when she discovered Little House on the Prairie by Laura Ingalls Wilder. She wrote her first book, a mystery, at age thirteen and has been writing ever since. She loves all animals, especially dogs, cats, and horses, and they often find their way into her books.

She has written twenty-two books, including books in the Beach Brides series, Moonshine Madness series, and West Loon Bay series. Her books have hit the Top 100 Bestseller list on Amazon, and she has been listed on Amazon's Top 100 Authors.

If you'd like to know more about her, visit her website at:

www.deniseannettedevine.com

Keep scrolling for more books by Denise Devine!

More Books by Denise Devine

Christmas Stories
Merry Christmas, Darling

A Christmas to Remember

A Merry Little Christmas

A Very Merry Christmas - Hawaiian Holiday Series

~*~

Sweet Romance
The Encore Bride

Lisa – Beach Brides Series

Ava – Perfect Match Series

Della – Enchanted Island Series

~*~

Moonshine Madness Series - Historical Suspense/Romance
The Bootlegger's Wife – Book 1

Guarding the Bootlegger's Widow – Book 2

The Bootlegger's Legacy – Book 3

~*~

Charlotte Van Elsberg Mystery Series
The Nightengale Detective Agency – *Coming Soon!*

~*~

West Loon Bay Series – Small Town Romance
Small Town Girl – Book 1

Brown-Eyed Girl – Book 2

Country Girl – Book 3 - *Coming Soon!*

~*~

Christmas in West Loon Bay Series– Small Town Romance
Once Upon a Christmas – Book 1

Mistletoe and Wine – Book 2

~*~

Cozy Mystery

Unfinished Business

Dark Fortune

~ Girl Friday Cozy Series ~

Shot in the Dark – Book 1

The Accidental Detective – *Coming Soon!*

~*~

Forever Yours Series - Inspirational romance

Always is not Forever – Book 1

This Time Forever – Book 2

Want more? Read the first chapter of my novels or get my complete book list at:

https://deniseannette.blogspot.com

~*~

Audiobooks Galore!

Do you like audiobooks? Many in the list above are available in audio! Check out Denise's website for links to each audiobook.

https://www.deniseannettedevine.com

Narrated by Lorana L. Hoopes

Monthly sales!

~*~

Passionate about sweet romance?

Want to be part of a fun group?

Visit us on Facebook at:

Happily Ever After Stories – Sweet Romance